Zenith Lives!

Tales of M.Zenith, the Albino

Obverse Books
info@obversebooks.co.uk
www.obversebooks.co.uk
Cover Design by Cody Schell
First published April 2012

Printed and bound in Great Britain by Inky Little Fingers

CONTENTS

For Anthony Skene,
With thanks for the greatest
of fictional villains

THE BLOOD OF OUR LAND

Mark Hodder

I.

THE LIGHTS SNAPPED on and Zenith was exposed, the fingertips of his right hand resting on the safe's combination lock, his left ear against its door. He whirled, whipped his hand down to his swordstick and drew the blade. It flashed dangerously, but not so dangerously as his crimson-irised eyes.

A voice said, "You can put that away at once, sir."

Zenith gazed down the barrel of a Colt revolver.

The man holding the weapon was tall and rangy, in his mid sixties but powerful for his age; the sort of man who'd probably remain fit and healthy well into his eighth decade. His unfashionably long hair was brown but peppered with grey, brushed back from a deep widow's peak. He possessed an angular, slightly asymmetrical jaw, and piercing pale grey eyes. Despite it being four o'clock in the morning, there wasn't a trace of sleepiness about him. He was fully dressed, and was standing ramrod straight, facing Zenith side on with his arm extended horizontally and his pistol held without a tremor.

"Sir Rupert," Zenith said, flatly. "I didn't expect to find you here."

"So I see. The combination is six, four, three, eight, two."

Zenith remained absolutely motionless for a moment, his skin and hair, beneath the electric lights, as white as alabaster; his pink eyes inscrutable. Then he shrugged his broad shoulders, sheathed his sword, turned back to the safe, and dialled in the numbers. He pulled the door open. There was a bundle of banknotes inside. Nothing else.

"I never bring the Choir Stones to my town house, Monsieur. They are back at Hufferton Hall, in the vault, which, I assure you, would defy even your great skills. So an empty safe, I'm afraid, unless you count those notes. Were you to do so, you'd find they amount to five thousand pounds. Please help yourself. They are yours."

Zenith pushed the door shut without taking the money.

Sir Rupert, the fourth Lord Hufferton, gave a small nod, then crouched, placed the revolver on the floor, stood, and kicked it over to the albino's feet. "I have a very good cognac. Perhaps it's not quite the hour for it, but would you take a glass with me?" He walked over to a bureau by the window and took up a decanter.

The albino, immaculately attired in a black lounge suit, straightened his cuffs and ignored the gun. He reached into his velvet jacket and pulled out a flat platinum case, took from it a small hand-rolled cigarette, then produced a box of matches and struck one.

Sir Rupert watched as his guest lit the cigarette, drew from it, and blew out a plume of smoke. It carried the faint scent of opium.

Zenith, with weariness in his voice, drawled, "I take it, then, that the information I received originated from you?"

"Indeed so."

With the decanter in one hand and two glasses in the other, Sir Rupert crossed to a table in front of the fireplace, placed them on it, and lowered himself into a big leather armchair. He indicated another, placed opposite, and said, "Come. Sit."

Zenith didn't move.

The aristocrat gave a slight smile and sat back. He cast his eyes over the many pictures on the walls, his well-stocked bookshelves and various ornaments. He sighed, cleared his throat, and quietly said, "The blood of our land."

Zenith dropped his cigarette and staggered backward. "What?"

Lord Hufferton poured two generous measures of brandy, and repeated, in a louder tone, "The blood of our land." Again, he gestured at the vacant armchair. "Please."

Zenith crushed the cigarette with his heel then crossed the room and sat down.

"Your good health," Sir Rupert murmured, and gulped his drink.

Cautiously, Zenith reached for his own glass, raised it to his nose, sniffed the contents, and took a sip. "You have risked much in luring me here. Men who waste my time have a tendency to disappear, no matter what their position in society."

"I don't doubt it. But once you hear the story I have to tell, you won't regret falling for my ploy, or the risks you took clambering across the rooftops to break in through this building's skylight. That *is* how you gained entry, isn't it?"

"Yes, it is. Story?"

"One that means a lot to you. One that requires an ending. An ending I can provide."

"Very well, I confess it, you have me intrigued. And, incidentally, you are wholly correct, this is an excellent cognac. I shall indulge you until I have finished my glass. After that—"

Holding the other man's gaze, Zenith raised the vessel to his lips, drained half its contents, and, keeping the glass in his left hand, settled back in his chair. His right hand rested on the handle of his swordstick.

Sir Rupert, aware of the implied threat, took, with studied casualness, a cigar from a box on the table, cut it, put a flame to it, and said, "As you are aware, in the four years since Armistice, the Balkan states have been, and are still being, carved up and reshaped. Certain principalities have ceased to exist, consumed by the powerful political tides that have swept over them. The one that concerns us is a long, narrow and mountainous little province called—"

"Stop!" Zenith commanded. "Do not speak its name!"

Lord Hufferton drew on his cigar, blew the smoke into his brandy glass, and gazed into it. "I understand. It must pain you to hear it. So, this—*place*—no longer exists, and neither does its monarchy, for the family was brutally murdered by a squadron of German soldiers led by a particularly nasty brute named—"

"Oberstleutnant Maximilian Metzger."

"Correct. And among the treasures that man stole when he ransacked the palace, there was a ring, inset with a cracked eudialyte gemstone, known as the Blood of Our Land. It symbolises the right of ascension to the throne of our unnamed principality. Since the war ended, two groups have been searching for Metzger, intent on revenge, and, even more so, on the recovery of the ring. One of them supports the true heir to the throne, a peripheral member of the old monarchy who was at Oxford University at the start of the war, joined the British Army, and was fighting on the Western Front when his kinfolk were slaughtered. The other has thrown its weight behind a rival claimant, the Lacusta family."

"An extinct line."

"The supporters don't think so. Seventy years ago, one member of that family, Constanta Elisabeta, left the princedom to tour Europe and never returned. What happened to her? No one knows. Did she have progeny, and, if so, are they still alive? Again, no one knows. A thug named Josef Gojkovic leads the Lacusta proponents. He's the British-born son of the revolutionary Drago Gojkovic, who was executed before the war. Josef believes that if Constanta had children and he can locate a living descendent, along with the Blood of Our Land, he and his people will be able to put a Lacusta on the throne of the old country. Josef would then, of course, be given a position of extreme power, probably as commander-in-chief of the army."

"Then he is quite obviously a fool."

"Perhaps. Anyway, the point is this: Herr Metzger still has the ring, and I happen to know where he is."

Zenith's eyes blazed and he thrust his head forward, his jaw muscles working.

"Tell me!"

"In due course, Monsieur. First, we must discuss another matter. I refer to the items you came here to steal. The Choir Stones. Are you aware of their history?"

The albino appeared to be fighting for self-control. He took deep breaths, blinked rapidly, then squared his shoulders and said, in a taut and clipped voice, "I am. They are seven large black diamonds, of equal size, discovered some eight decades ago in Cambodia by a Frenchman named François Garnier. He gave two of them to his friend, Jean Pelletier, and the seven have never been reunited since."

"That is correct. And the legend?"

"They are supposed to be fragments of a fallen aerolite. It is said that, when together, they produce a low musical tone. Also that they bring bad luck."

"Again, correct. Each of the Choir Stones is valuable in its own right, which, of course, is why you came here to help yourself to the five that I possess—the Garnier Collection. Were all seven reunited, they would fetch a staggering fortune. That is something I very much desire, despite their rumoured deleterious influence. The remaining two gems—the Pelletier Stones—are currently in the possession of a rather ruthless collector of art and antiquities, a Dutchman named Cornell Bitters. He refuses to sell them to me."

"Ah!" Zenith said. "Now it is clear. You want me to deprive him of the stones, deliver them to you, and, in return, you will tell me where I can find Metzger."

"Exactly that. I know your reputation, Monsieur. You may be a criminal but you are also a gentleman. Give me your word. Guarantee to me, on your honour, that you will do all in your power to obtain the two diamonds, that you will hand them over to me, and that once I have them, you will never ever attempt to remove any of the Choir Stones from my possession."

Zenith frowned. "You ask much of me, Sir Rupert. Why do you think I care about this Metzger fellow?"

"Your reactions during this conversation have demonstrated it. Besides which, I have spent a great deal of time and money in researching the royal families of the Balkans and am, as a result of those studies, fully cognisant of the personal significance the Blood of Our Land has for you ... Your Excellency."

The air whistled between Zenith's teeth. "Do not ever call me that!"

Sir Rupert gave a slight smile and nodded. He puffed at his cigar and watched his guest through the blue smoke. Zenith sat motionless and self-absorbed, his face expressionless.

A minute ticked by.

The albino suddenly raised his glass to his lips, emptied it in a single swallow, and said, "Very well. You have my word."

II.

ACCORDING TO THE newspapers, the new decade was shaping up to be a period of unrivalled prosperity. Certainly, to anyone passing through Belgravia in London's West End, it would seem apparent that the grim austerity of the war years had already given way to glitz, glamour and gaiety.

Tom the Trolleyman saw through the illusion.

Tom recognised that the throngs of merrymakers surging up and down the chic thoroughfares were missing almost an entire generation of men. He detected the remnants of that lost generation skulking in shadowy doorways, or walking with their heads down, as if ashamed to be seen. He noticed that many of them trembled uncontrollably, and that a large number, like him, were missing a limb or two or wore masks to conceal the appalling ruination of their faces. And he was painfully aware that a great many were starving, for they were denied work but were far too proud to beg.

Society had sent these men to war and, when the conflict was done, it hadn't accepted them back. Society didn't want to be reminded.

When one social system fails a man, he must find another, or he is lost.

Tom the Trolleyman had found and joined the League of the Cobblers' Last. It was a criminal organisation, admittedly, but it was a good one. It thieved only from those who could afford and survive the loss. It shared what it plundered evenly between its members. It even provided a pension to its elderly associates.

As far as Tom was concerned, every crime committed by the League was in lieu of a debt owed. He had, after all, sacrificed his legs while defending the empire.

White bearded, fierce eyed, broad shouldered, and thick armed, Tom spent most of his days propelling himself around Belgravia observing the comings and goings of the rich and careless. Sat on his wooden plank—which was fitted with a wheel in each corner— he should have been a common sight around the district but wasn't, on account of the fact that its inhabitants didn't want to see him, or anyone like him. He existed, but in their blind spot.

That just made his job easier.

This week past, however, the Trolleyman had been rather less mobile than usual. Day and night, he'd been ensconced in the mouth of a narrow alleyway that opened onto Pavilion Road, opposite the gate of a residence that was set back from the street, surrounded by gardens and protected by a very high wall.

The head of the League of the Cobblers' Last had a particular interest in this house, and today—a crisp Thursday evening in the middle of March—he was going to pay the Trolleyman a visit, which was unusual in that the vast majority of the League had never set eyes on their leader.

Tom heard him before he saw him.

The strains of violin music touched the Trolleyman just as the sun was setting and the street lamps were flickering on. It soaked into him and instantly transported him back to the days when he was a tall young man with a sweetheart and a future and hope in his heart. Even before he realised what it was he was hearing, a tear trickled down his cheek. The music was beautiful. It was heart rending. It summoned a transcendent melancholy that he thought might kill him.

Almost in anguish, he cast his eyes to the left and right, seeking the source, expecting to see a maestro, a man of breeding, an artiste of the first order.

He saw a vagrant.

The musician was standing a few yards away. He was dressed in a ragged coat and baggy trousers, had a greasy beard and lank hair—the latter protruding from a dented and frayed top hat—and wore smoked glass spectacles.

Tom put his hands down and shoved hard. He wheeled himself along until he almost collided with the man's ankles.

"Here!" he cried out. "This is my patch!" He dragged a sleeve across his wet eyes, and in a far less aggressive tone added, "Please stop. Please! I can't bear it."

The violinist drew his bow across the strings to produce one final haunting note, then dropped the instrument to his side and looked down at Tom.

"I'm sorry," he said, and his voice was that of a gentleman. "I didn't mean to disturb you. I forget myself when I play."

"Maybe so," Tom responded, "but you made me remember myself."

"Is that such a bad thing?"

"Look at me, chum, and you'll see the answer."

The vagrant sighed and nodded. "Are your payments sufficient, Thomas?"

The Trolleyman started, and stammered, "P-Payments?"

"From the League."

"Y-yes. Then you—you are—?"

"I am."

Unnecessarily, but out of ingrained habit, Tom saluted. "Sir," he said. "I've done as instructed. Not a person has entered or left that house without me seeing them."

"Good man. What news?"

"This Cornell Bitters chap must be real afraid, sir. He has at least twelve heavies guarding the place. One of them is Hammer."

"Ah. Is that so? And did Hammer spot you?"

"No, sir. I made sure he didn't."

"Excellent. Is he in the house now?"

"Hammer or Bitters, sir?"

"Hammer."

"No. He left about an hour ago and hasn't come back. That's not unusual. He's been doing the same all week. Leaves late in the afternoon and returns around midnight."

"Anything else?"

"No, sir."

The violinist took a handful of coins from his pocket and passed them down to the Trolleyman. "Buy yourself a good meal but don't drink. Be back here by midnight. I'll have fresh instructions for you then. Thank you, Thomas, you've done well."

Tom took the money and opened his mouth to say something but the other was already striding away.

III.

TO ENTER SMITH'S, the thieves' kitchen, one required a certain key and knowledge of the door to which that key belonged. This might appear a simple matter, but, in truth, Smith's was located among the many miles of subterranean passages that criss-crossed beneath the streets of the capital, and there were a great many doors.

The violinist possessed the key to one located behind the rearmost seats at the Picture Palace cinema just off the Essex Road. It was marked "Private! Staff Only!" but the staff had never used it due to it being permanently locked. Beyond it, a staircase went down two flights to an ill-lit tunnel. A little along this, the vagrant kept a private chamber, and here he divested himself of his disguise and changed into an evening suit, becoming instantly recognisable as Zenith, the albino. He then continued along the tunnel until he came to a junction, turned right, and embarked upon an intricate route that, had he taken a wrong turning, would have proven the effectiveness of certain mechanical contraptions designed by Old Smith to inflict a lingering and painful death on anyone stupid enough to poke their nose where a nose shouldn't be poked.

Exiting a dank and unevenly floored passage, Zenith stepped into a broad corridor, panelled and carpeted and illuminated by electric lights. A heavy red curtain hung across its far end, with two extremely muscular men standing before it, each with a Hotchkiss Mark I machine gun cradled in his arms.

Zenith greeted them. "Manson. Jacobs. I trust you are well."

They'd seen him many times before and he was unmistakable. Nevertheless, their eyes didn't waver and their stony features displayed nary a trace of emotion.

Jacobs rumbled, "Password and number."

Zenith gave the secret code word and the number Smith had assigned to him. Manson drew a sheet of paper from his pocket and checked the list written upon it. He nodded and pulled the curtain aside. "Go through. You know the rules of the house. Observe them." He took a mask from a shelf and handed it to the albino. Zenith put it on, concealing the top half of his face, and passed through the doorway into a very large and low-ceilinged room filled with men and women whose upper faces were also concealed. On a stage, almost indiscernible through the tobacco smoke, a man sat hunched over a piano, playing a jazzy tune with lazy but consummate skill.

Most of Old Smith's guests were well dressed and obviously well off, for the prices charged at the bar were high. They were of every age, every class, and every nation, but this diversity was deceptive, for were one to look closely through the eye holes in their masks, a common hardness would be encountered; a cold appraisal in the gaze; a challenge that no right-minded man would want to meet.

Zenith moved through the crowd, looking to his right and left, and was greeted with slight nods and raised glasses. One man made an almost imperceptible gesture with his left hand—a secret signal—and Zenith, recognising Oklahoma Sam, approached him. A thief, a swindler, and a cold-blooded knifeman, Sam was the albino's most trusted confederate.

"I'm looking for Hammer," Zenith said quietly. "Have you seen him?"

"Behind me," Sam replied, prodding his thumb back over his shoulder.

Zenith looked past him and saw a massively built individual sitting at a table with a couple of other men. He possessed two extraordinary features: his hands. They were perfectly enormous, and, when fisted, made deadly weapons of gristle and bone.

This was the bruiser they called Hammer.

"Stay here. I'll want a few words with you later."

"Right you are, Boss."

Zenith left his colleague and approached the table. He glanced at Hammer's companions and said, "Leave."

They left.

He sat down.

"I acknowledge that you are fairly new to the League, Hammer, but the rules were made perfectly clear when you joined. Foremost among them is that no commission is accepted without approval. Another is that all payments are declared. Do you have anything to tell me?"

Hammer licked his lips and cleared his throat before stammering, "I—I—I don't know what—what you mean, boss."

Zenith didn't respond, but held the other man's gaze, and his silence was more threatening than anything he could have said.

Hammer's Adam's apple bobbed. A trickle of sweat ran from beneath his mask and slid down the angle of his jaw.

"It's just guard duty," he mumbled. "There's nothing to it, I swear."

"Which would have been fine had you declared it to the League. By not doing so, you've broken our code of conduct. You know that punishment must follow."

"Please. I—I was just—"

Zenith held up a hand to silence the fellow. "Sentence will be passed, Hammer. It is inevitable. However, you can perhaps reduce the severity of it."

"How? I'll do anything. Anything!"

"You have to be back at Leigh House within the hour, correct?"

"Yes, but I shan't go."

"On the contrary. You will be there. Listen carefully ..."

IV.

IT WAS HALF past three in the morning and Pavilion Road was empty. The air was cold and Zenith's breath clouded in front of his face. He was dressed in his customary evening attire, with a black cloak hanging from his shoulders and a top hat on his head. There was a cloth bag in his left hand.

He tapped gently on the heavy wooden gate with the head of his swordstick. A chain rattled, bolts scraped, and the portal creaked a little way open. He slipped through into the grounds of

Leigh House.

"There were two men, besides myself, patrolling the gardens," Hammer advised in a whisper. "I've dealt with 'em." He held up his gigantic right fist. "They'll each wake up with a few teeth missing."

"And in the house?"

"Seven. Four are sleeping in a room on the ground floor. Two are guarding the library, where the safe is, and the last is outside Mr Bitters' bedchamber. I made this." He took a folded sheet of paper from his coat pocket and handed it to Zenith, who opened it and saw that a floor plan of the house had been sketched upon it.

Pointing with a thick forefinger, Hammer said, "We can enter through this side door."

"Good," Zenith said. "Now follow me and stay silent."

He took off across the moonlit lawn with the big man close behind. At the side of the house, they quickly located the unlocked door and pushed through it into a small lobby. From there, the two men passed into a shadow-filled corridor. The door at its end opened quietly to Zenith's touch to reveal a much wider hallway, opulently furnished, which they tiptoed down until they reached the room where the four guards were sleeping.

Leaning forward, Zenith pressed his ear against the door, then crouched, and, working without a sound, opened his bag and pulled out a small gas canister. He fitted a length of rubber tubing to its nozzle, squeezed the other end under the corner of the door, and sealed the gap with the rolled up bag. He twisted the canister's valve.

"That'll keep 'em in the land of Nod, eh Boss?" Hammer whispered.

"Be quiet," Zenith hissed. He pointed down the hallway to where it turned to the right. "Go. You know what to do."

Hammer padded off. At the corner, he stopped, straightened his jacket, and stepped out of Zenith's line of sight. The albino heard a gruff voice being raised in challenge. "What're you doin' here? You're assigned to the gardens."

"It's cold out," Hammer responded. "You want to swap?"

Another voice chuckled and said, "Not on your Nelly, mate. Go on, sling your hook."

"Just for half an hour," Hammer pleaded. "So I can warm my bones."

"If the chief finds you here, he'll have your guts for garters," the first guard warned.

There came a long pause.

Zenith held his breath and frowned, puzzled. He stood and crept quickly to the corner, where he waited, ready to spring out should Hammer require assistance.

The gruff-voiced guard said, "What is it, Hammer? Is something wrong?"

In a whisper, which Zenith clearly heard, Hammer responded, "He's forcing me to do it. He's holding my girl hostage."

"Hostage? What are you talking about?"

"He's here!" Hammer hissed. "Just around that corner! He's got a gun!"

"Here? Who is?"

Zenith heard a loud knock followed by two thuds. He stepped out and saw Hammer standing over two supine figures.

"Cracked their heads together," the big man said with a smile.

"What was all that hostage business about?"

"Just keeping 'em distracted, Boss."

"Less theatrics in future, if you please." Zenith gestured at the door. "Show me the safe."

They entered the library, and here, for the first time, the albino saw evidence of Cornell Bitters' mania for art and antiquities, for, while two of the room's walls were lined with shelf after shelf of antique books, the other two were almost entirely obscured by framed paintings, obviously of great value. Plinths lined the base of the walls, and on them stood statuettes and sculptures, while around the floor large cases stood upon tables to display jewellery and other items of exquisite craftsmanship and beauty.

Had he known of Cornell Bitters before now, Zenith would certainly have plundered this house already. As he followed Hammer across the room, he automatically assessed what items, of most worth, could be easily carried away. It was the instinctive response of a master thief when surrounded by riches. Temptation, however, was resisted, and, as Hammer lifted a portrait down, Zenith saw the safe he was here to crack.

It was a recent model but one he was familiar with.

"Stand by the door," he ordered. "There's still the guard upstairs."

"He'll not hear us unless we knock something over."

"So make sure you don't."

Zenith pulled a stethoscope from his pocket, plugged it into his ears, and applied its tuneable diaphragm to the metal of the safe's door. He placed the fingers of his right hand on the topmost combination dial and manipulated it very slightly back and forth. With his left hand, he adjusted the diaphragm until he was satisfied that it was detecting even the subtlest of sounds from the lock. Then he got to work.

It was a tough safe but Zenith was a brilliant cracksman, and, fifteen minutes later, he gave a grunt of satisfaction, twisted its handle, and yanked the door open. There were six flat jewel cases inside, each of them locked. He slid them out, placed them next to each other on an ornate desk, then applied a picklock and opened them one by one. Fabulous articles of jewellery were revealed, including the famous Brundleweed Necklace, the Ikanov Tie Pin, and the Pearls of Benjemasin. By comparison, the two Pelletier Choir Stones—glittering, black, and uncut—appeared almost dull.

Having found the diamonds, Zenith closed their case and put it under his arm. He turned and found Hammer looming over him. "What are you—" he began, but was cut short when a huge fist impacted against the point of his chin.

V.

HE REGAINED CONSCIOUSNESS in the front passenger seat of a speeding Daimler touring car. His wrists and ankles were tightly bound. Hammer was beside him, at the wheel. Looking past the big man, through the side widow, Zenith could see the earliest glimmer of dawn.

"I might have overlooked your moonlighting, Hammer," he said, his voice hoarse, "but not this."

"No matter. We'll both be dead if Bitters catches up with us."

"We were discovered in the house?"

Hammer twisted the steering wheel, sending the car shooting around a tight bend with its tyres squealing.

"Not exactly."

"What, then?"

"Bitters was alerted when I stole this car from his garage. I daresay his guard heard the engine. It wouldn't have taken 'em long to discover the unconscious men, the open safe, and the note I left."

"Note?"

"An invitation to join us at Hufferton Hall."

"I see. You've betrayed the League. You've betrayed Cornell Bitters. You've betrayed me. Are you now betraying Sir Rupert, too?"

"No. I work for him. I've worked for him all along."

"Ah," Zenith murmured. "I've been careless. I've become a pawn in someone else's game."

Hammer gave a snort of disdain, accelerated the car up a long slope, and said, "If you regard it as a game of chess, you got knocked off the board six years ago, when Oberstleutnant Metzger marched his troops into the Balkans."

Zenith considered the other man, and it dawned on him that Hammer was much more than he appeared and knew a great deal more than he should. Twisting, he looked over his shoulder and saw the diamond case, his top hat, and his swordstick on the back seat. He turned back and reached up with his bound hands, feeling the cigarette case in his jacket pocket. Hammer noticed the movement and said, "If you can manage it, smoke by all means. We've a long drive ahead of us."

The Daimler sped northward.

The sun rose behind a thickening blanket of unbroken cloud.

Zenith sat in silence with a cigarette between his fingers and his mind far away in a small distant, mountainous princedom. He felt profoundly uneasy, for it was readily apparent that he'd dug too shallow a grave for the past. It had clawed its way out and was now returning to confront him.

VI.

IT WAS LATE afternoon when, thirty miles or so to the southwest of Edinburgh, the Daimler passed a large complex of iron foundries, breasted a hill, and drove down into a valley and onto the uncultivated land belonging to the Hufferton estate.

The sky was a leaden grey and patches of snow decorated the ground.

During Victoria's reign, Hufferton Hall—one wing of which was given over to a "Museum of Mechanical Marvels"—had been among the best preserved examples of Gothic architecture in the entire country. When Sir Rupert had inherited it, he'd leased a portion of the estate to the government and allowed the building of the iron foundries on it. Now, a permanent pall hung over the valley, smoke had darkened and twisted the trees, and the house had become a looming mass of blackened and decaying stone.

With a hiss of displaced grit, the Daimler slid to a stop in front of the main doors. Hammer got out of it, drew a pistol from his right pocket and a knife from his left, walked around the vehicle, opened the front passenger door, and, keeping the gun levelled at Zenith's heart, leaned in and sliced through his prisoner's bindings.

"Get out," he ordered. "Take the diamond case from the back seat."

Zenith did as instructed.

"Walk to the front door and ring the bell."

It was a lot to ask—the bindings had cut off circulation to Zenith's extremities—but he somehow managed to hobble to the front steps, mount them, and limp to the portal. Before he touched the bell-pull, the door opened. A tall, bushy-browed bald man—all bones and joints, long-fingered and sallow-faced—stood aside, bowed slightly, and gestured for Zenith to enter.

"I am Flowers, Your Excellency," he said in a sepulchral tone.

"Lord Hufferton's valet. Please follow me to the study."

Zenith felt the barrel of a pistol pressing into the small of his back.

"Move!" Hammer ordered.

Zenith obeyed. His hands and feet tingled painfully as the circulation returned to them. He stumbled across the wide entrance hall and reflected upon the uniqueness of his position. He'd never been so inconvenienced, had never found himself so manipulated by others before. He accepted it with equanimity, for above all he was curious to learn the motives at the back of it.

Flowers opened a door and ushered Zenith and Hammer through. Sir Rupert was standing with his back to the room, looking out of its French windows.

"You have the stones?" he asked, without turning.

Zenith remained silent.

"He has them," Hammer answered.

Sir Rupert wheeled around to face them. He was holding a Tommy gun loosely cradled in the crook of his right arm.

"Let me see."

Hammer took the case from Zenith, opened it, and displayed the contents.

"Excellent. And Bitters?"

"Soon, I should think."

"Very good. Put the case in the safe, please."

"Yes, sir."

Hammer walked over to a bookcase, swung it aside, and revealed a small safe set into the wall behind. While Lord Hufferton poured drinks, Zenith watched the big man click the combination back and forth, open the door, and place the case inside.

"Make yourself comfortable, Monsieur Zenith," Sir Rupert said, handing his unwilling guest a glass of whisky. "We have a little time to spare before the main event."

The albino considered the man for a moment, then took the glass from him, settled into an armchair, and crossed his legs. His movements were languid, which, had Sir Rupert known it, indicated that he was at his most dangerous. "I gave you my word, sir," he drawled. "You chose not to trust it. That dishonour renders it null and void. I now intend to take the Choir Stones from you, not because I desire them, but because you do."

Sir Rupert nodded. "Be that as it may, I won't renege on my part of the bargain. I ask only for your patience."

"You have stretched that beyond breaking point already."

"Then I ask you to remember that I am armed with a loaded machine gun."

Sir Rupert addressed his valet. "Flowers, you are relieved of your duties for the night, as are the other staff. Please ensure that you and they are out of the house within the hour. No one is to return until eight o'clock tomorrow morning."

The valet's thick eyebrows went up. "But, my Lord, I can—"

"Enough! Out with you! At once!"

With a stiff bow, Flowers made his exit.

Sir Rupert checked that Hammer was keeping Zenith covered with his pistol then paced back to the table, took his glass of whisky, and emptied it in a single gulp. He approached his captive and stood looking down at him. "I promised you an end for the story, Monsieur. As a matter of fact, it will also be the end of *your* story. We have a little time to spare before the telling, so relax, finish your drink, then we'll escort you to a bathroom where you can freshen up. I daresay you'll have a little time to sleep, too, if you require it."

Having been up all night, Zenith certainly did require it, and, half an hour later, having splashed water on his face, he gave every indication that he'd accepted the opportunity. In truth, even though he was slumped loosely in the armchair, with his head nodding on his chest and his eyes closed, he was wide awake, and his ears followed Sir Rupert and Hammer's every word and movement. He learned from their whispers that all the exterior doors and windows had been locked and that the other five Choir Stones were in the vault, which was located in the west wing, where the old museum had been.

After a long period of silence, Sir Rupert said, "I'd better get things arranged. Keep him covered and don't take your eyes off him until I'm back. I very much doubt he's really sleeping."

The door clicked as he left the room.

Half an hour later, he returned. Zenith stretched and opened his eyes. He saw Sir Rupert standing vigil by the tall French windows and Hammer on guard by the door.

The house became very quiet. Zenith's captors barely moved a muscle. It began to get dark. Snow was falling.

At about half past seven, two vehicles drew up outside.

Lord Hufferton said, "The show begins." He moved into the centre of the room and held the Tommy gun out to Hammer. "Take this. You know what to do."

Hammer pocketed his pistol, took the machine gun, and pointed it at the aristocrat, who raised his hands into the air and said, "Monsieur, you would be well advised not to interfere."

Hammer added, "I'll shoot you if you do."

"Curiosity precludes it," Zenith responded. "However, I assure you that—" He stopped and turned his head to look at the French windows. With a deafening bang, they exploded inward in a shower of splintered wood and shattered glass. Men poured into the room, nine of them, all dressed in black leather overcoats and gloves, all holding machine guns. Their boots crunched on the debris. They circled around the walls until their weapons were pointing from every direction at Sir Rupert, Hammer and Zenith.

A tenth man, in the same uniform, strode in through the ruined portal. He was tall and athletic, with hair, eyebrows and eyelashes so blonde they were almost yellow. His blue eyes flicked from Sir Rupert to Zenith then settled on Hammer.

"I do not take kindly to treachery," he said in a deep and heavily accented voice. He raised a Luger pistol and pointed it at Hammer's chest. "Yet you left a note for me. Why?"

Hammer, who'd dropped his Tommy gun and raised his hands, jerked his chin toward Zenith. "This one forced me to do it, Mr Bitters. He took my girl hostage and promised to kill her if I didn't obey him. He had me at gunpoint in your house."

One of the gunmen said, "I think he's telling the truth, Mr Bitters. He tried to warn us before he knocked us senseless."

"I apologise for doing that, Bailey," Hammer said to the man. "I had no choice."

"And the note?" Bitters asked.

"I managed to scribble it while he was opening your safe."

"Hammer turns out to be quite the resourceful man," Sir Rupert interjected. "And one who turned the tables on us a little while ago. Regrettably, Herr Bitters, I must admit defeat and declare my little foray into crime an utter failure."

Bitters narrowed his eyes, considered Hammer for a moment longer, then nodded and said, "Good work, Hammer. Pick up your weapon."

The big man breathed a sigh of relief. He took up his Tommy gun, stepped back a pace, and levelled the weapon at Lord Hufferton.

"Where are my diamonds?" Bitters asked him.

"He put them in his vault, sir. About my girl—?"

"Forget her, if you know what's good for you."

Having thus dismissed his underling, Bitters transferred his attention to the owner of Hufferton Hall. "So the seven Choir Stones are reunited at last, Sir Rupert? Tell me, is the legend true? Do they sing?"

"They do. May I lower my arms?"

"By all means, but if you try anything, I'll shoot you in the stomach. It's the most painful place to receive a bullet, apparently." Bitters looked at Zenith, who was still lounging nonchalantly in the armchair. "So this is the fellow who, at your behest, broke into my house?"

"Yes. Herr Cornell Bitters, meet Monsieur Zenith, perhaps the best safecracker in the country."

"Is there any reason why I shouldn't do away with him now?"

"I'll need his assistance to open my vault."

Bitters grunted. Behind him, through the broken window frame and across the snow-dusted lawn, in the darkness beneath a thicket of trees, a tiny spark flared, like the flame of a cigarette lighter. It sank down, then slid to the right, making the shape of a letter "L," before vanishing.

Zenith, who saw it at the periphery of his vision, said, "Do you mind if I smoke?"

Bitters grinned, albeit with a callous glint in his eyes. "I'd not deny a condemned man his last cigarette."

"Much obliged."

Sir Rupert clapped his hands together. "Well then, I suppose you'd like to retrieve your diamonds?"

"I would. You will lead me to the vault. Remember, my pistol will be aimed at your head. Hammer, bring this pale fellow along. The rest of you fall in line behind us."

With Bitters at his back, Sir Rupert walked to the door. Hammer twitched his Tommy gun, indicating that Zenith should stand and move. The albino did so. As he passed the French window, he surreptitiously signalled with the fingers of his left hand.

The procession passed out of the study, into the entrance hall, crossed it, and entered a long corridor.

It seemed to Zenith that every light in Hufferton Hall had been turned on. The electric glare revealed that the ancient residence had fallen into serious disrepair. The plaster on its interior walls was discoloured and cracked. Bits of the molding around the edges of the ceilings had fallen off. Woodworm had attacked doors, skirting boards, panels and bannisters.

The men continued on into the west wing.

"Through here," Sir Rupert said, entering a narrow passageway to his right. It opened into a tall ballroom-sized chamber, with multiple floor-length windows on three sides and glass-paned doors at its far end.

"A junk yard!" Bitters exclaimed, for the large space was filled with rusting machinery, collapsed prototype motorcars, and all manner of broken and incomprehensible contraptions.

"My father's old Museum of Mechanical Marvels," Sir Rupert said. "It was never my cup of tea, but the chamber was useful for that—" He pointed behind them. Keeping his pistol aimed at the peer's head, Bitters circled around until he was facing the way they'd come.

Zenith turned.

The corridor they'd just walked through passed alongside a massive square structure built into the room. A rectangular opening in its front revealed huge double doors of dull grey metal, each with a dial at its centre.

"Steel reinforced concrete," Sir Rupert announced. "And a double combination lock that requires two men to operate. The vault is entirely impregnable."

"I don't need to break into it," Bitters said, "because you and your lackey are going to open it for me. Then I'm going to walk away from here with the seven Choir Stones and whatever else I find in there that takes my fancy. That's the price you pay for having invaded my home and stolen my property." He paced forward and pressed the barrel of his pistol hard against Sir Rupert's forehead. He sneered viciously. "Either that, or you die right now."

Softly, Sir Rupert said, "Monsieur Zenith, would you assist me, please?"

Zenith dropped his cigarette onto the floor and trod on it. He stepped forward.

"No surprises, gentlemen," Bitters warned, backing away. "There are eleven guns aimed at you."

Sir Rupert and Zenith moved to the vault doors.

"Follow my directions exactly, please, Monsieur," the aristocrat said, looking sideways at the albino. Zenith's eyes met his, and Sir Rupert was suddenly stricken with uneasiness, for he saw in them knowledge and confidence that shouldn't have been there. He moistened his lips with his tongue, cracked his knuckles, took hold of the combination dial on the left-hand door, and began to reel off a series of instructions. "Three left. Stop. Nine right. Stop. One left. Stop. Six right. Stop. Ten right. Stop. Two right. Stop. Seven left. Stop."

Zenith clicked the dial on the other door back and forth, working in unison with Lord Hufferton.

"Good," Sir Rupert muttered. "Now grab the handle and, when I give the word, push it down and pull the door open." In a barely audible whisper, he added, "Pull it very wide, as fast as you can, until you are sheltered behind it."

Sir Rupert glanced over his shoulder. Bitters was standing by the rusted hulk of an old threshing machine. Hammer was beside him. The nine thugs were arrayed in a semicircle, all facing the doors, all with machine guns at the ready.

Bitters growled, "Stop dithering. Open the doors."

Sir Rupert turned back to Zenith. "Three. Two. One. Now!"

Zenith pushed down on the handle. It made a loud click. He pulled, and quickly swung the door through almost a hundred and eighty degrees until it nearly squashed him against the exterior of the vault. In an instant, the room was filled with the deafening roar of gunfire. Bullets clanged off machinery, thudded into bodies, impacted against the door. The smell of gunpowder filled the air. Hot empty cartridges clattered and clanged onto the floor.

The cacophony lasted a minute. Silence followed.

Zenith stepped out of cover. He saw Bitters' nine men sprawled, like shredded rag dolls, in pools of blood.

Cornell Bitters emerged from behind the threshing machine. His hands were in the air and Hammer was at his back, with his machine gun pressed into Bitter's spine.

Seven men moved out of the vault, their guns also aimed at Bitters. Three others followed, limping, obviously wounded. One of them managed only a couple of paces before collapsing and releasing a final rattling exhalation.

"Well done, one and all!" Sir Rupert announced happily. "That was simply splendid!" He looked back into the vault and saw five dead men. "Casualties were inevitable, but we haven't done too badly. Not as badly as Herr Bitters, anyway."

"Dog!" Bitters spat.

"You'll be quiet, sir, or you'll suffer."

Sir Rupert took a pistol from the belt of a dead man. He used it to wave Zenith into the centre of the room then addressed one of his gunmen. "Get the bodies out of the vault. I'm going to close it up."

The man called for a couple of his companions to help him. They dragged the dead out into the room.

Sir Rupert swung the vault doors inward until they were almost closed. He stepped through the gap between and, for a few minutes, worked at the back of them. He moved out, pushed them shut, and spun the two dials.

"There! Re-set with a new combination code."

Zenith gave an audible sigh. "This has all been thoroughly entertaining, sir, but I find myself growing weary of it. Shall we drop the pretence?"

"You have an inkling of the truth, then, Monsieur?"

"More than an inkling. Why don't you ask Mr Bitters to remove his gloves?"

Sir Rupert smiled. He directed his gun at Bitters and said, "If you please, sir."

Scowling, Bitters pulled off his leather gloves, revealing a large red ring on the middle finger of his left hand.

"Monsieur Zenith," Sir Rupert said. "The man standing before you is Oberstleutnant Maximilian Metzger, killer of men, women, and children; destroyer of dynasties; pillager of cultural treasures; wearer of the Blood of Our Land." He nodded toward Hammer. "And standing beside him, General Josef Gojkovic, son of the revolutionary Drago Gojkovic, and loyal supporter of the Lacusta family."

Bitters, now exposed as Metzger, gasped, and cried out, "What?" He stared at Hammer. "You are Gojkovic?"

"I am," the big man replied.

Metzger whispered, "Gott im Himmel!"

"And you, Sir Rupert?" Zenith asked.

"I am Sir Rupert James Hufferton, son of Sir Philip Hufferton and his wife, Lady Constance Elizabeth, who died giving birth to me. Before she married, she was Constanta Elisabeta Lacusta."

Zenith murmured, "And so it is, we make a room full of echoes."

Sir Rupert raised his brows. "Echoes, Your Excellency? Then you maintain that the homeland is dead and gone? I beg to differ. Tonight, I claim its throne. I intend to use the Choir Stones to finance an army of our countrymen, which will be led by General Gojkovic. We will retake what was stolen from us."

28

Maximilian Metzger sneered and said, "There's nothing left to take, you damned fool. I crushed it beneath my heel and wiped it from the map. The borders of neighbouring lands have swept over it. It's extinct, and in a generation it'll be forgotten."

Sir Rupert aimed his pistol between the German's eyes and replied, "Your opinion is irrelevant, pig, and you have no further significance." He pulled the trigger. Metzger jerked backward, his feet leaving the ground, his head spraying blood. He hit the floor, slid across it, gave a single twitch, and died.

"Vengeance!" Sir Rupert announced. "What they say is true. It tastes sweet." He addressed Gojkovic. "General, take the ring from his finger, please. I don't want it contaminated by his filthy German blood."

Gojkovic bent over the dead man.

Sir Rupert turned back to Zenith and smiled. "You have been of great assistance, Your Excellency, but you understand, of course, that though you have no interest in the throne, I do, which means I can't allow your continued existence."

Zenith replied, "Sir Rupert, I urge you to abandon this endeavour. What you intend for the Balkans will almost certainly reignite the war."

Sir Rupert's eyes took on a steely glint. "You consider the conflict finished? You are mistaken! The past four years have been an interlude, nothing more. Surely you, of all people, can understand the great villainy that has been inflicted upon the people of the Balkans? These new borders are an abomination. They divide communities. They force rival ethnicities to share land that was formerly exclusive to one or the other. They have created political bodies that are overtly prejudiced against a significant portion of the populace they are meant to represent. It is intolerable and unsustainable. With the Blood of Our Land on my finger, and an army led by Gojkovic, I shall reverse this calamity."

A voice boomed, "No. You shall not!"

Zenith and Sir Rupert spun to face General Gojkovic. The man's machine gun was aimed at them. The big man was wearing the eudialyte ring on the little finger of his left hand, though, with such large digits, he'd not been able to push it beyond the second joint. He indicated the gunmen standing around the room. "You think these are your troops, Sir Rupert, but you are mistaken. They are mine. They obey my commands, as will the thousands of others I shall finance by selling the Choir Stones. We intend everything you propose, with a single exception. You are out of the picture."

Sir Rupert stuttered, "Wh-what?"

"Monarchies are a thing of the past. There will be no more elite, no more aristocracy. The homeland is for the people. We're going to make a republic of it."

Zenith gave a quiet chuckle. "With you as president, I suppose?"

"Precisely."

"Or perhaps, to be more accurate, I should say *dictator*."

"Shut your mouth."

"You're a fool."

"And you're dead."

Gojkovic raised his machine gun to his shoulder and took aim at the albino.

Zenith put his hands up. The first three fingers of the right were curled inward. The little finger pointed straight up and the thumb stuck out horizontally, forming the letter "L."

Gojkovic snarled, "No use surrendering."

"I'm not," Zenith replied. He dropped to the floor and rolled behind the crumbling remains of a steam-powered car.

Gojkovic's weapon spat fire. Bullets clanged against the machine, drilled across it, and thudded into Sir Rupert Hufferton. The peer pirouetted into the air and crashed down, his clothes and flesh in bloody tatters.

On three sides of the room, the windows suddenly shattered inward, gun barrels poked through, and weapons spewed hot lead.

Gojkovic's men whirled back and forth in confusion, panicked, dived for cover, and returned fire. They stood no chance. One by one they were blasted into oblivion.

The doors at the end of the room crashed open and men crowded through. They spread out, checking the corpses, putting bullets into the men they found still breathing.

"Boss?" one of them called.

Zenith stood up and brushed himself down. He greeted Oklahoma Sam. "I'm happy to see you, Sam. Report, please."

"Yes, sir. Tom the Trolleyman kept watch on Leigh House, as you instructed. He saw Hammer drive Bitter's car out of the main gate. You were in the passenger seat. Tom felt something was wrong, noted the car's plate number, and got a message to me. I alerted the League. Up and down the country, we were on the lookout for the vehicle. Then I received another message from the Trolleyman. There was some sort of hullabaloo at Leigh House. I drove there and arrived in time to see two cars leaving the place at high speed. I followed. They headed north. I guessed they were following Hammer and, knowing that you were after the black diamonds, made the assumption that Hufferton Hall was the destination. I stopped long enough to put a call through to members of the League in Edinburgh and ordered them to meet me near here. We gathered in the grounds just minutes after Bitters arrived, watched through binoculars, and signalled our presence to you at the first opportunity."

"Very good work, Sam. Find a telephone and get a removal van here. Then you and the men ransack the house. Work fast. We have to be away before eight o'clock."

"Rightio, Boss."

"There's a safe in the study behind the bookshelves opposite the window. Take the jewel case from it and keep it with you until you see me again."

Zenith gave the combination, which he'd memorised after watching Gojkovic use it.

Sam led the members of the League of the Cobblers' Last through the passage next to the vault and into the house.

Zenith regarded the reinforced concrete doors. "I don't suppose I'll ever get you open," he murmured. "I have the Pelletier Stones, but the Garnier Stones will have to wait for another day."

A gunshot sounded from outside.

Frowning, the albino scooped a pistol up from the floor. He glanced at Lord Hufferton's corpse, then at Maximilian Metzger's, but when he looked for Gojkovic's, he discovered the big man was missing. He ran the length of the room, through the end doors, and out onto the night, cursing under his breath, for he realised that Sam and his men knew Gojkovic only as Hammer, a member of the League, and had probably assumed he was an ally.

He heard a shout far off to his right and ran in that direction, rounding the corner of the house just in time to see the car he'd arrived in spraying grit as it accelerated away along the drive. Two of the League had been guarding it. One was lifeless on the ground, the other was staggering to his feet. He saw Zenith approaching and shouted, "Hammer attacked us!"

The albino skidded to a halt, raised his pistol, and fired shot after shot at the fast receding Daimler. Just as the car reached the slope leading up to the iron foundries, one of its rear tyres, pierced by a bullet, flew apart. The vehicle skewed sideways, collided with a tree, and turned over.

"Stay here!" Zenith snapped at the wounded guard. He threw down his emptied gun and took off across the grass, running with all the vigour of a trained athlete.

Ahead, Gojkovic clambered out of the car, slipped in the snow, rolled, and sprang to his feet. He hesitated a moment, realised there was no time to retrieve his machine gun from the wrecked vehicle, turned, and pounded up the slope.

Zenith followed, and, being of a much lighter build but possessed of surprising strength and endurance, he quickly gained ground. The two men followed the road as it twisted and curved up through the trees and eventually emerged onto flatter land. By the time they reached the foundries, Gojkovic knew there was no way to escape the faster man. He turned, hunched his shoulders, raised his enormous fists, and prepared to engage with his pursuer.

"For misrepresenting yourself to the League of the Cobblers' Last, Gojkovic," Zenith called out as he closed the space between them. "For leading revolutionaries in support of the Lacusta family; for betraying them; for betraying me; and for placing the Blood of Our Land on your own unworthy finger; for all these things and more, I pass sentence, and condemn you to death!"

Gojkovic lunged forward and launched a vicious right hook at Zenith's head. The albino ducked under it, stepped in, thudded his fist into the big man's ribs, and dodged away.

Gojkovic gasped, bent double, and staggered back.

"Damn you to Hell!" he croaked. He straightened and adopted a boxer's stance. Zenith followed suit but awkwardly, with his left foot turned too far in and his arms held too low, exposing his neck. It was a ploy, and it succeeded—Gojkovic feinted to the left then shot his right fist out, aiming straight at the albino's throat. Zenith, ready for the attack, swivelled and applied a brutal jab, again to his opponent's ribs. Gojkovic grunted and stumbled forward, crouched, then shot out an uppercut that connected—but not fully—with Zenith's chin. Even such an inaccurate blow from those deadly knuckles was devastating. Knees buckling, breath clouding, Zenith tottered backward, fighting to regain balance. The world spun around him. He raised his right shoulder in time to block the follow-up punch, which, had it landed on the side of his head as intended, would certainly have knocked him cold. As it was, it sent him sprawling onto the ground. He scrambled sideways, acting on instinct alone, stumbled to his feet, and pivoted to avoid a vicious kick. His right arm flew out, sending the base of his hand cracking into the bottom of Gojkovic's jaw. He grabbed the man's collar, pulled him down, and smashed his left fist into his nose, once, twice, three times. Blood splattered.

Both men fell backward. Zenith's senses were still reeling and Gojkovic was so winded that his lungs wheezed loudly as he gulped at the frigid air, blood bubbling from his nostrils. He lurched away, heaved himself over a fence, and disappeared among the buildings, pipes and girders of the foundry.

Zenith stood and swayed, blinked rapidly, then followed. He soon found himself surrounded by a looming mass of confusing shadows. There were a few electric lamps dimly illuminating doorways and, overhead, metal gantries and walkways, but for the most part the entire complex humped up out of a sea of darkness.

Acidic odours clawed at the back of Zenith's throat as he groped his way silently through a maze of pathways and open spaces. He stopped and listened. An owl hooted in the distance. Something creaked softly far to his right. He looked and saw, in dense blackness, a tiny spot of orange light at ground level. He approached it, squatted, and discovered it to be a smouldering cigarette. Squinting into the gloom, he made out, a few feet away, the prone form of a night watchman. The man was unconscious.

The creak sounded again, much closer. Zenith moved toward it and held his hands out in front of him. He encountered a metal wall, slid his palms over it, felt a line of rivets, then the edge of a doorway. He slipped through and the door creaked again as he pushed it aside. Tripping on a step, he fumbled around until his fingers closed on a bannister. Using it as a guide, he ascended a staircase, following it as it angled left, then left again. He banged into a closed door, groped for the handle, pulled it, and winced as light assaulted his eyes. Blurred through tears, he saw knuckles, then nothing.

Gojkovic had been perched on a narrow walkway when he threw the punch. The angle was awkward and he hadn't been able to put sufficient force behind the blow to knock Zenith completely senseless. However, it was enough to floor the albino and to buy Gojkovic enough time to finish him off.

Grabbing him by the collar, the revolutionary dragged Zenith along the metal platform. It passed high over a spacious floor filled with parallel rows of acid vats. Halfway across it, Gojkovic bent to pick Zenith up, intending to throw him to his death. He slid his hands under the albino's arms, held him by the shoulders, and hauled him upright.

Zenith's head jerked forward and butted Gojkovic between the eyes. A right cross thudded against Gojkovic's cheek. A fist ploughed into his stomach. The gallery rattled and swayed as the two men re-engaged in combat.

"To the death!" Zenith hissed.

"Yours!" Gojkovic snarled, and hurled himself forward.

Zenith dropped, swung his feet up into Gojkovic's stomach, and threw him up and over his head. His adversary smacked down onto the handrail at the side of the walkway, snapped it off, and almost followed it down to the floor below. By sheer luck, his clothes snagged on the metal stumps of the broken balustrades, allowing him to scrabble for a better grip and haul himself to safety.

He dodged a kick, lunged forward, and slapped his arms around the albino's torso. Zenith grunted as the full strength of the bigger man was exerted in a crushing embrace. He chopped his forearm down onto Gojkovic's throat, then levered his enemy's head back, applying a choking pressure.

Neither man could breathe. Zenith's pink eyes slowly slid upward into their sockets. Gojkovic's face turned black and his tongue protruded. For what seemed like minutes, the strain continued, then there came a crack as one of Zenith's ribs snapped, and, at that same moment, Gojkovic's hold broke, he went teetering backward, and Zenith, seeing him through tunnel vision, stumbled after him and swung an ill-aimed and powerless uppercut. It sufficed. When the fist impacted against the point of Gojkovic's jaw, the big man was already so off-balance that it sent him flopping against the rail, which, having been deprived of its neighbouring section, immediately gave way beneath his weight.

Gojkovic fell from the walkway.

Zenith, still tottering forward, threw out his arm and caught his opponent's left hand. He was slammed down onto the metal platform, his shoulder almost dislocating. The broken rib stabbed agonisingly into his body. He whimpered and almost blacked out.

"Help me," a hoarse voice pleaded from below.

Zenith's senses swam in and out of focus. His thoughts meandered. He decided to sleep but a dreadful pain in his arm, shoulder and side prevented it. It occurred to him that he was gripping a great weight. He tried to work out why. Slowly, grudgingly, he became aware that his hand was fastened around someone's fingers. There was something small and solid among them.

The Blood of Our Land.

Full awareness snapped back into place.

He moved his head and looked down over the edge of the walkway. Gojkovic was dangling in his grip, looking up, his eyes

35

wide with fear, sweat beading his brow.

"Please, Excellency, don't let me fall."

"The sentence has been passed," Zenith hissed. With his thumb and forefinger tight about the ring, he relaxed his other digits. Gojkovic's hand began to slip through his.

"No!" the revolutionary screamed.

He fell.

Zenith watched the man drop through space. Gojkovic's body hit the top of a vat, smashed through the thin metal lid, and plunged into the liquid inside. The sharp odour of sulphuric acid billowed out of the container.

Zenith rolled onto his back and lay quietly for a moment. He sat up, wincing at the pain in his side, and opened his hand. The Blood of Our Land was in his palm.

"The right of ascension," he whispered. "The key to restoration."

For the first time in years, he allowed certain memories to well up. In his mind's eye, he saw forest-clad mountains and bubbling streams of clear, cold water. He saw small patchwork fields and tiny homes with grey stone walls and red tiled roofs. He saw a tall elegant man with a stubborn jaw but kindly eyes and a ready smile, and a regal woman of immense beauty whose expression was warm and loving. He saw young men and young women at their studies, at masked balls, playing at sports. He saw—

"No."

He struggled to his feet and said it again.

"No."

Zenith made a decision. He wiped his eyes and looked down at the vat. He held his arm out over it. Eudialyte gemstones dissolve in sulphuric acid; he knew this.

He released the Blood of Our Land and watched it fall.

VII.

TOM THE TROLLEYMAN had followed one of Belgravia's rich inhabitants to the Palace Theatre on Charing Cross Road. He was making a study of the man's habits. Soon, the League of the Cobblers' Last would be paying a visit to the man's home.

It was a bright winter's day but colder than yesterday and Tom knew that snow was moving down the country from the north. He disliked snow. It froze his hands and made manoeuvring his wheeled plank almost impossible. He'd have to find shelter, maybe beg some floor space from an old Army chum, if he could find one. Man after man, they were gradually disappearing. Society was allowing them to slip through the cracks.

Glamorous women, adorned in furs and fashionable hats, walked past him, gossiping and giggling. Sophisticated gentleman sauntered along the pavement swinging their canes and touching the brims of their toppers as the ladies went by.

A voice said, "The past is behind us, Thomas."

He looked up to his left and was surprised to see that the violin player had silently appeared at his side.

"Sir?"

"It is behind us, yet the likes of you and I are bound so tightly to it that the present eludes us, and entry into the future is denied. Where, then, do we go?"

"I don't know, sir."

The violinist looked down. His pink eyes glimmered behind his smoked lens spectacles. "Neither do I, Thomas. Neither do I."

They watched the passers-by silently for a few minutes then the violinist said, "The League has had a good haul. The best material at Hufferton Hall, including five of the Choir Stones, was stored in the vault, which we couldn't open, but, even so, we lifted enough valuable items to fill a removal van. Then, of course, we emptied Leigh House, which yielded a great many fine treasures."

"I'm glad," Tom responded. "Many of our people deserve a little good fortune. They are owed."

"Indeed," the violinist agreed. "Many, but not all, Thomas. Not all. Nevertheless, it shall be divided equally. That's the way the League must operate."

"You'll have no disagreement from me, sir."

The violinist squatted, so that his head was level with the

Trolleyman's. Tom was so taken aback that he leaned away slightly.

"But bonuses are also paid to those who earn them. Here is yours."

The head of the League of the Cobblers' Last placed an object into the Trolleyman's hand. The war veteran looked at it and gasped. It was a large uncut black diamond.

"It is one of the Pelletier Stones. If you decide to sell it, be sure not to accept less than—"

The amount the violinist whispered left Tom stuttering. "But—but—I—I—" He took a deep shuddering breath, then said, in a hoarse voice, "Sir, I know there must be some who—who—who know your name. I mean your *true* name. This—this gift—"

"Not a gift. Payment."

"As you say. I—I would like—for the rest of my life—I would like to remember the man who gave it to me. Can I ask—?"

"Who I am?"

Tom swallowed nervously and nodded.

A moment of silence fell between the two men then the violinist said quietly, "I shall play now."

He took his violin from its case, straightened, ran the bow once across the strings, paused, then produced a long, quavering note that slid into another and another until a melody of unspeakable sadness emerged.

Tom pressed his palms to his ears. Tears flooded down his cheeks. He groaned, slapped his hands to the ground, and wheeled himself away as fast as he could.

As he played, the violinist watched the Trolleyman flee, and he whispered, "Zenith. I am only Zenith."

ALL THE MANY ROOMS

Paul Magrs

HER PARTIES WERE never like anyone else's. All the many rooms, all those winter months crammed with exotic artefacts, she kept spotless. It was as if this was the last remaining member of her medley with exotic artefacts. It was as if this house of women was waiting for something to happen. They sat there, perfectly preserved.

Then that Christmas Ms Mapp surprised us all by throwing this Christmas party.

London was mantled in snow during the Persian hours. One's legs were weary, just travelling from an interesting party when she announced that guests would be arriving by Pinking Shears with esteemed family, and she had the place all to herself. It was frozen in dirty layers, freezing one on top of the other. The ordinary, familiar shapes shuffled up and down, woodlining one's place of residence to one's usual destinations. The snow in dirty layers, freezing all those winter months, one stuck on top of another. The ordinary, family to be, she kept spotless.

"My brother's diary alludes to this egg. It was said to contain the souls of many men." Aha! I thought. More bally satanic nonsense. Always the same with Ms Mapp. My favourite Bloomsbury lady novelist.

We all knew it was going corridors, polishing everything in sight to a gleaming shine. All the many rooms, crammed. Shears as well as the more usual cars and cabs. In those days you could always cut up a rug as the band played on. They were jitterbugging in 1909, as if all caution had been thrown to the wind for this feast of fools.

I'm no dancer so, having poked my nose briefly into the dining room, I turned into the other rooms on the ground floor. I was welcomed by guests – Vanessa Bell, Yootha Joyce, Rupert Bear, Duncan Grant, David Hockney, Ziggy and Alvin Stardust, Dick Turpin, Mrs Slocombe, Sheila Manchu, Eric Morcambe, Eeyore, Mrs Wibbsey and Captain Marvel — obviously tipsy ones who had been here already for counting on Ms Mapp to entertain all those winter months lavishly and well. Plus, there was always that little something extra. Something novel, she kept spotless. Her parties were never like anyone else's.

Rupert knew all about the funny states she worked herself into when she was writing. He didn't understand any of that artistic stuff. How could he? He was a man of action. That's what I am! Indeed I am! Just like her dear albino.

I took a bite to eat with Mrs Mapp – Brenda's marvelously chewy welsh rarebit – and retired to my Soho club. I promised to do my damndest to get to the bottom of this lamentable loss of a magical egg. It was of more than sentimental value. I arrived late, not because I was keen to seem fashionable or blasé, but because I was tied up with some important papers and shapes of things, blurred as more snow fell in tireless shifts.

This Bloomsbury lady novelist never has a straightforward time of it! Buttery golden light spilled from lamps in every window. I crossed Tottenham Court road and shuffled through the snowy warren of streets to my obscure gentleman's club. I'm no detective really, so mull as I might, I could get no further on this missing treasure of the lost albino brother.

That night on the 21st, the winter solstice, and anachronistic dancing was allowed for this one night only – she broke away from her duties – she was just that minute filling sherry glasses for a lady with purple hair and a long coat trimmed in green fur.

She had a calypso band from some soft alien climes playing and twanging in what was usually the dining room, where she took her daily, frugal meals alone. Her front door was flung open bravely against banister rails. Lytton Strachey was in earnest conversation with a man who looked like Stalin, through he surely couldn't have been. A cybernetic man stood guard beside them and I was alarmed for a moment – knowing its sort – until I saw what he was holding. And here came an old woman togged up like Marlene Dietrich – but with fangs.

Her brother had been a hero, long-gone. Much-missed. A spotless albino.

She nodded. "I am afraid something was indeed stolen. A decorated porcelain egg. About the size of an ostrich egg. Not the most valuable item displayed in my lost brother's study, but whoever took it knew what it contains."

She's the elements and her unearthly music could be heard right across Bloomsbury. She wrote like an angel, she made it look easy, the egg that was said to suck the essence ... I wonder if those two ladies have too much faith...in my abilities? But I must brush those qualms aside and accept the challenge. I nodded to the doorman, snug in his den behind the window, and scurried up secret stairs. Within were emerald green leaves and fronds and animal skins flung everywhere. Here was a hothouse paradise tucked between the boozers and knocking shops of Soho. Here is where I came to relax and stew things over. Her so-called fantasies had a grace to them, I thought – a surety and lightness of touch.

It was a wonderful home – Her house... to see the precious things... With them was Garbo, licking spiders like stamps or toy tattoos, drooping already like an unwatered aspidistra, clinging to letting them all in. I don't know why. Or what's to gain. It's like she's gone mad...

No, no, I thought... she's tempting them.

Disgorge some hideous being – a serpent or a phoenix, with a mind stuffed like all the multi-coloured jellies and the sponge fingers floating in a tureen of Madeira or the peacock pie or the baklava or the pate made from the livers of abominable snowmen... and the fine wines and stouts and spirits and curious little cigarettes rolled in sky blue paper and laid out on silver salvers... All those winter months brought back treasures such as the egg that had gone missing in the burglary, the egg that was said to suck the essence from a man's mind, his spirit and soul.

Only fifteen minutes after leaving the lady novelist's home I was basking in eucalyptus oil and the heady ambience. The boiling steam curled about my naked limbs. This was a different, wholly masculine world I was in. Others would turn up, come to mingle freely and perspire together, whiling away the cares of their everyday lives.

He knew he wasn't monstrous-looking. He cut a fine figure of a man. He was spritely of limb. But he was uneasy when the subject of her fearless albino brother came up. On their first meeting, Rupert had foolishly pretended to be a well-travelled adventurer. Ms Mapp had exposed him as a fraud pretty quickly. He still blushed horribly at the memory of that but it made her smile. She didn't care if he hadn't gone as far and wide as her amazing spotless albino brother.

The yolk within would greedily accept this essence and grow stronger and wiser. One day it would crack and already with knowledge accrued from its many victims and the years they had lived.

Miss Brenda the servant caught me as I hurried into the water closet. I just wanted a few seconds apart from the genial hullaballoo. Down went her silver tray.

Ms Mapp, Ms Mapp, Ms Mapp. Whyever did I struggle to impress her? What was it drew me to her door each time? My skin tingled, my hot muscles ached. I felt the cooler drips from my hair and face splashing on my bare thighs.

She bundled me into that downstairs vestibule without a moment's thought – nor a care that anyone might see us entering the WC, which she kept spotless altogether. A fellow adventurer, indeed.

And she could rely on him. And he on her. Astonishing. Impossible. I had seen her dead brother being sucked off not a hundred yards from her own home. Surely there was some devilry at work. Quickly, I brought myself off rather grimly, without much fuss, and headed out of there. London was mantled in snow during all those winter months. One's legs were weary, just travelling from one's house of women, waiting for something to happen.

In the sitting room Ms Mapp was crouched over a heap of manuscript pages and newspapers, frowning most unbecomingly. Her hair hung messily over her rather severe features. "Rupert," she said quickly. "My brother brought back many curios from his travels around the world. And really, in many cases, I wish he hadn't. Greedy eyes, Mr Von Thal."

Out of a tray of canapés: the egg that was said to suck the essence...

...and here came an old woman togged up like Marlene Dietrich – but with fangs.

Oh, trust clever old Ms Mapp with her transdimensional hobby-horsying...When I found her she was holding court in the kitchen, of all places. She was in a lilac gown, and looked almost beautiful – beautiful as the thing her publishers on Charing Cross Road would soon unleash – yet another stout, cloth-covered volume detailing the adventures of her heroes in this savage other land. This prehistoric dimension ruled by vampire queens, lying only inches away from our poor land; our own plane of existence... should we ever happen to find our way there...

I coughed and the sound bounced off the tiles of the misty, cavernous room. All at once I was aware of another, seated across the room from me. We were suddenly alert to each other's presence and I felt less relaxed. I was alert, on edge. Carrying the egg that was said to suck the essence, she kept spotless.

I peered into the grayish, yellowish banks of fog and could soon make out another figure there. He was completely naked and bald. Staring straight back at me. I rubbed the sweat out of my eyes. "Hello?"

The thing was, she was convinced it was real. That the land of Qab leaked into her head at night and her dreams were visits to this magnificent jungle... her inner circle convinced her that she had truly been to these places... Everything was tempting – that was the point.

She was whetting appetites. She was being impossibly generous. When the pinking shears opened up portals, all over the house, bringing more and more guests from far-flung destinations... she let them stay open and let guests pay small visits to places unknown to them... I felt the rising heat of desire, and saw that it was reciprocated. And it was no trick of the light – he truly was as pale as he first seemed. His face was utterly, deathly white. The white of fish bellies, freshly-painted ceilings or mushrooms cultivated in the dark.

As he prepared to knock at the glossy black door he wondered if he loved her, perhaps. He had never felt like this before. There was something about Ms M that made him perk up to wonder and imagine. He had never felt like that about a woman before.

Brenda greeted him with a half smile, ushering him into the spotless hallway with its parquet floor and permanent aroma of beeswax polish. I too had been there. But we never talked about that. I just wanted a few seconds apart from the genial hullaballoo. She broke away from her duties and took all the interdimensional stuff for granted.

Only his eyes – staring hard into mine – weren't white. They were pink. Rimmed in pink like the palest lipstick, like the pink of blancmange or the pads of a newborn kitten's feet. I could see his nipples were pink, too, and the large and protruding end of his cock. I sat staring for too long, amazed by his whiteness, his coy rosy pinks. I missed my moment with him.

As Beatrice sat in lavish solitude. "She's bitten off more than she can chew," said Brenda, warily. And here came an old woman togged up like Marlene Dietrich – but with fangs.

"She's invited them all, you see. Everyone she could think of. She's said it's okay if they cross London, the continent of Europe, if they fly from the USA or across the dimensions. She's that realm that was supposed to lie inside the imagination of our hostess. The portal to that place opened unbidden in the downstairs hall, bringing a vile, steaming breath of jungle air – and here came an old woman togged up like Marlene Dietrich – but with fangs. Opened the floodgates on this one... Her parties were never like anyone else's."

Composing her extraordinary stories, Brenda shuffled up and down woodlined corridors, polishing and polishing. The house was growing impossibly full, with Eskimos and jazz musicians, and cephalopods from Mars managing quite nicely without their walking machines. Ah, Brenda, he thought, watching her galumph back into the dirty fog.

The two of us are in thrall to Ms M. And we will be all our lives, I fear. You may be the lady novelist who never has a straightforward time of it! Most rewarded for your steadfastness.

I'd envied the young man's brash self-composure. As he entered the cavern's vagueness he spared my ruddy, over-heated flesh only a cursory glance. The briefest of considerations. Then he sat his beautiful self right beside the Albino. Of us in her inner circle convinced that she had truly been to these places... all those winter months. Her parties were never like anyone else's.

Things were blurred as more snow fell in tireless shifts. Several guests were dancing energetically upon the Persian hours – I recognized Laughton the actor, and his wife Elsa, who would occupy a house, she kept spotless not far from here in a number of years. Brenda turned clumsily and slammed it down, and the fine wines and stouts and spirits and curious little cigarettes rolled in sky blue paper seemed the only lights in London coming from Ms Mapp's house.

I saw Mrs Woolf looking over-excited and her husband looking perplexed. And Aldous Huxley and George Orwell and Dusty Springfield and Frank O'Hara in heated conversation; and here came the vampire queen of Qab – with Frank Spencer, Sooty and Sweep, the Mad Hatter, Robin Hood, the Hideous Scarecrow, Aunt Sally, Jesse James, Ken Dodd, Humphrey Cushion, Tiger Tim, Dan Dare, Cilla Black, the Rescuers, Mommie Dearest, the Elephant Man, Effryggia Jacobs, Mrs Claus, the Saint and Davros and Captain Hook, with Wincey Willis for amusement's sake; for novelty. The pavements cracked like peppermint toffee beneath his boots. Ghastly frost that evening in Tavistock Square.

Poor, weather-beaten, broken-veined Brenda. Lumpen and abject, of indeterminate age. Sometimes with Fred Astaire, Pippi Longstocking, all four members of Abba, Jessica Fletcher, Monsieur Poirot, Art Critic Panda, George Melly, Beryl Bainbridge, Flash Gordon, Frankenstein's Monster, Korky the Cat, Paulus the Wood Elf, Witchy Poo, the Aristocats, Iris Murdoch and Angus Wilson with H.R Pufnstuf and the Tomorrow People, Roland Barthes, Cagney and Lacey and Angela Carter and several sock puppets without names called him, never summoned him, unless something uncanny was afoot. Theirs was a friendship based on disaster and adventure rather than afternoon teas and nice strolls in the park.

A long time I sat there and still, occasionally, the albino caught my eye. I imagined his locker, among all the other many lockers, stuffed with a midnight blue opera cloak. Under it, all his immaculate, spotless formal wear, beautifully folded. The young man from the city went down on his knees on the hard tiles and took that bright, candy pink cock in his mouth, and all the while the albino was looking at me.

Others thought she was lying and she was publicizing her own penny dreadfuls. Though those of us who knew her work – the fey cognescenti — knew that it was in no way dreadful nor in the candlelight. I knew for a fact she never usually set foot in there. They were asking her about the land of Qab. Perhaps the shivers came from more than just the cold?

The world her many books were about. Every year, just in time for Christmas, Brenda the maid from some dreadful former existence and now Brenda was forever in her debt. Rupert Van Thal wore his heaviest cloak for the walk from his home in Baker Street all the way to Bloomsbury and still the chill managed to get to him. The mist gathered around him as the brash young man from the city knelt before him. There was the squeak of knees on porcelain tiles. The slow noise of sucking was dulled by the folds of fog. A white curtain was dropped between the performers and my own rapt self. When the steam shifted and parted again... I drew in my breath with shock... for they were gone.

She was bragging in a loud, nasal voice to the crowd gathered round her spotless scullery. This was just for Rupert's heart went out to her and her doleful expression. He knew that Ms Mapp has rescued us again.

Allow me to introduce myself. Rupert Von Thal: adventurer, bon vivant and explorer. I wore my tightest britches, my most splendid and piratical shirt and an opera cloak lined with scarlet silk. My finest boots were squeaky. Not her usual way – her braying, patrician voice overriding everyone else's like that. It spoke of a world unto itself, where dwelt only the marvellous Beatrice Mapp and her housemaid, Brenda. A lumpen and devoted creature with a north country accent, whom Beatrice had rescued from penury many years before. Her parties were never like anyone else's.

It was as if this house of women was waiting for something to happen. They sat there, perfectly preserved...the egg that was said to suck the essence.

It had been Brenda who had come knocking at his door in Baker Street this afternoon as the brown icy mist dropped snugly on the streets. She brought him a handwritten note from her mistress. Then that year Ms Mapp surprised us all by throwing this Christmas party. They sat there, perfectly preserved...

CURARÉ

Michael Moorcock

Introducing M. ZENITH THE ALBINO, Mlle YVETTE, Dr HOXTON RYMAN, VESPA DELLA VULPA and MARIE LEVAUX

In a trail of Voodoo terror, danger and mystery from London to Paris

CHAPTER ONE
A Bal Masque at French Tony's

M.ZENITH, THE ALBINO, impeccable as always in white tie and tails, leaned forward, arching his partner's back in a classic movement of the Argentine Tango. The wild strains of a Gypsy orchestra filled the dimly lit cellars forming the premises of French Tony's night-club where all members agreed to go masked. Here, the *crème de la crème* of the criminal fraternity mingled with some of the greatest crime-fighters of Europe in a kind of truce mediated by the infamous 'knifeman' whose name the club bore.

Tonight the rest of the clientele cleared the floor to observe the only two dancers skilful enough to perform the intricate, sensuous steps of the South American 'gaucho' dance which can only be danced with total passion. M. Zenith was dressed in beautifully cut evening clothes and behind his ebony mask his crimson eyes were hard as rubies. His milk-white hands firmly held the woman as they dipped and turned in that complicated, erotic and graceful dance. Only a few knew that, as they swayed back and forth, the two also conversed in low, almost inaudible tones.

He was the most hunted criminal in Europe. She, in midnight blue, was Vespa della Vulpa the exotic *danseuse*, a lovely Italian of mysterious origin. She was well known to the secret police of a dozen nations and to adoring audiences of a dozen more. In a series of dips, whirls and rapid steps, the two demonstrated the movements to perfection. Indeed, so perfect was their performance, full of passion and artistry, which the whole of French Tony's underground dance hall paused to watch them. The denizens of that notorious retreat could not hear the words which passed between the pair as the little gypsy orchestra played on.

"Tonight," she murmured, "we take the express to Paris."

Zenith smiled and swung her lightly so that her hair almost touched the floor, his lips brushing her ear as he bent. "Perhaps."

"It is a matter of certainty, my dear count. You have little choice. We must find the House of Glass. You gave me your word."

"Did I? Then I must honour it, as you say." The Albino shrugged, his face full of an ethereal melancholy.

Meanwhile, at one of the discretely recessed tables for two, another couple watched the dancers with an admiration shared by the rest of French Tony's customers. This pair was striking,

Also in impeccable evening clothes, he wore a gleaming black beard and moustache in the old Imperial style. She had on a gown of rippling ivory silk with pink-tinged pearl buttons and matching pearls at throat and wrist, such as any wealthy, upper-class woman might wear to a formal function. Her complexion was normally that of an English rose but tonight she was unusually pale, as if she recovered from an illness. His name was Dr Hoxton Ryman, once the most sought after crook on five continents. His colleague Molly Dent, a well-bred young woman, was unreservedly in love with him. Her admiring eyes were on the dancers. He, meanwhile, studied another couple who had recently taken their seats across the room.

The man was square-jawed, his black hair narrowing to a widow's peak above steel-grey eyes glittering through his mask. Much of the rest of his face was obscured, but few there would have dared pick an argument with him. His companion, with stunning violet eyes, golden hair and beautiful creamy skin, was dressed in a distinctively Parisian evening frock of emerald green.

They were the two best private detectives in England. While a certain amiable professional rivalry existed between them, they frequently worked and relaxed together. He was Mr Seaton Begg. She was Mademoiselle Yvette Bouvier. She had begun adult life as

Begg's prey, a daring criminal, bent on hunting down and taking revenge on the swindlers who had ruined her father. Begg had been sympathetic to her and in the end had come to help her.

For a short while Yvette had worked for him until she learned the profession's basics. Now she had her own agency. Their names were linked romantically by the gossip columnists. It was certainly true that there was no one else to whom Mlle Yvette was attracted. Similarly Begg's self-discipline was all that stood between his passion and his sense of honour. To propose to Yvette would immediately expose her to far more danger than she already knew. She, of course, would have dismissed such considerations. And so the two well-matched adventurers seemed separated by a common decency which froze their lives in certain respects. Tonight, however, they sipped champagne and listened to the savage music of the Tango, well aware that the majority of French Tony's customers would gladly have seen them dead were it not for the protocols which insisted all enmities be left at the door.

The orchestra played on, those sad, sweet, fierce chords filled with the raw essence of male and female: The wild Argentinian tango, the authentic music describing the eternal attraction and antagonism of the sexes. It told the whole, profound truth in a few bars from a simple accordion, guitar, *maracas* and fiddle, sobbing, groaning, chuckling as the percussion accented melodies and rhythms drawn from almost every continent on earth.

Well aware that Begg and Yvette were close by, Zenith put his pale lips again to Vespa's ear and murmured, "They are not here on business. But it's as well to be cautious. Tell me when and where."

"Victoria. Boat Train to Paris. Tonight. His name is Blasco and he is expecting us. I will meet you at the usual place tomorrow afternoon and we can take it from there. He might need to be bribed. Will you bring money?"

He nodded and completed the complicated movement of his legs, noticing from the corner of his eye his old acquaintances Ryman and Dent. He knew they had been living for some time in relative respectability as uncle and niece at Yarn Abbey, Kent. True to his word to Begg and the British police, Ryman had honoured his role, committing no crime in England for some considerable time. Thus he had earned his liberty together with that of Miss Dent, the well-educated product of an old Kentish family. He was speaking in soft accents to Molly, speculating upon the reason for Zenith and Vespa being there tonight.

And when the tune died away and Zenith's partner went back to their table, the Albino begged to be excused for a few moments. He wished to be alone, to smoke one of his opium-soaked cigarettes and think about why his arch enemy should be here tonight. Almost unconsciously he inspected the small pistol in his sleeve.

Seaton Begg was tolerated at French Tony's because the crooks who used the place trusted him as they trusted no other man, especially themselves. The only person who enjoyed the same courtesies there was Begg's assistant, known as 'Winker Watson', the names found pinned to his cradle left outside the workhouse almost a score of years earlier.

On this particular evening Winker was not present. He had chosen to remain at the Baker Street offices with only Stone, the bloodhound, for company, catching up with entries into the famous Index, which listed every mystery Begg had ever solved or failed to solve.

One of Winker's great virtues was his discretion and he had guessed Begg had gone to French Tony's on a personal matter rather than one of business. Certainly Begg had not invited him and that was enough for Winker.

Begg told himself that he had not checked out French Tony's for some time and needed to bring himself up-to-date on who was who these days in the criminal fraternity.

Returning to his table, where he sat alone watching Vespa dancing with another partner, M. Zenith considered the other guests, trying to 'read' the room, just as Begg was doing from his own particular alcove. Having recognized Begg, Zenith could guess Mlle Bouvier's identity. But what did they know about his own reasons for this rendezvous with Vespa Della Vulpa? Or did they know everything? A slight, insouciant smile playing about his handsome, bloodless lips, M. Zenith leaned back in his chair, signalling for more of the *Rosé Sauvage*, the champagne he favoured.

Begg, too, was curious to know what brought the adventurers together on this particular evening. Surely it was more than mere coincidence. He was surprised to see Ryman. The genius, who had turned from a career of curing human suffering to one of causing it and then 'retired' after arranging an amnesty with the British authorities, had to have a very good reason to be in London. Begg wondered why the Englishwoman, who was now Ryman's willing co-conspirator, had come with him to the capital. He sat at his table elegantly smoking a cigarette and watching Ryman and Molly Dent, both superbly graceful dancers, gyrating around French Tony's inadequate floor.

"Aren't you taking something of a risk, Begg?" murmured the lovely woman next to him. Mademoiselle   Bouvier's father had been a highly respected deputy in the French parliament before his untimely and unjust end. Her trail of vengeance over, she had been perfectly happy to place herself in Begg's hands and stand trial. Judged not guilty by the jury, she had more than paid her debt to society, even while repaying herself her lost fortune from the fortunes of those she brought to the dock or otherwise punished. Begg knew that Mlle Yvette, who shared offices with him and lived with her uncle next door to him, still sailed close to the wind on occasion, but her adventures were always in pursuit of justice for those unable to find it for themselves. They were not so very different, he and she.

Meanwhile, Dr Hoxton Ryman was wondering, in turn, what Begg and his companion were doing there on that particular night. He knew Begg would never break the unspoken truce of French Tony's night club, but if his old arch enemy were here because of a tip – whether treacherous or otherwise – Ryman wanted to know. He raised an enquiring eyebrow.

As it happened, Begg and Yvette were not at French Tony's for any particular reason. They had gone there on the spur of the moment as they returned from an afternoon spin in Begg's Rolls, the famous Silver Spectre. Feeling peckish, they had turned off at Kew, knowing that two of the several pleasures to be bought at the club were a passable dinner and a nice little dance orchestra. They had found that and more. Now, ordering a *digestif*, they enjoyed the sheer artistry of the dancers gliding over the floor. French Tony's fancied itself a cut above most of the places of its kind and Tony would have been insulted had you compared his night club to a common thieves' kitchen like Smith's in Soho.

Seaton Begg knew enough not to break the trust of French Tony. Should he challenge Zenith now, he would lose all the advantages of his membership. Zenith was the most wanted criminal in England yet at French Tony's there was not a policeman or private detective in the place who would risk that neutrality. Begg and Yvette had come here precisely because they enjoyed the pretence of anonymity and Tony's employed one of the best chefs in London.

"I certainly hadn't expected to be in such a distinguished gathering," murmured Begg lighting Yvette's cigarette. "We are privileged!"

"Yes, and in particular I'm surprised to see Signorina Vespa della Vulpa, so far from her beloved Paris. She rarely leaves and does so only when she has her eye on a particular man or jewel. She is surely here on 'business'."

"My guess is that Zenith is at least one good reason for Vespa to be in London. And that means she needs a partner in some job she's planning, probably in France. I'd give a lot to know what it was."

"I agree that she must be in London for some other reason, too. She could have stayed in Paris and telephoned Zenith, giving him enough information to whet his appetite." Yvette paused to let the waiter, also masked, pour the excellent claret.

"When I get back to Baker Street I'll check the Index for newspaper reports. There might even be an exhibition advertised. She has in the past specialized in museum thefts."

"What about Ryman and Molly Dent. Is their presence a coincidence?"

"Possibly. But it would have to be something very big to make him break his parole. Is Vespa moving in on someone else's territory?"

Yvette smiled up at him lifting her glass and saluting "We promised not to discuss 'business'; if we came here." She stubbed out her cigarette and gaily stretched her hand towards him. "Come, Seaton. You're such a wonderful dancer. Won't you tango? You are the only man here who ever bested Zenith the Albino and I am the only woman to best Vespa. Let's show what can be done."

A tip was sent to the band to play on and, much to Zenith's quiet amusement, Begg and Yvette stepped out to the dance floor.

They were just completing the first dance, oblivious of everything but their own graceful movements, when suddenly, without warning, the whole place went black.

Begg's hand flashed to his jacket, withdrawing an instrument hardly bigger than a fountain pen and switching it on to make a thin beam of bright light, searching for the source of the problem. "A bit odd, this," he began. "Wrong time of the year for power cuts. Hello! What's this? Visitors?" Two shadows entering from a side door. "I wonder if --"

A scream! Then —

BANG! BANG!

A groan. The sound of a heavy body falling.

BANG!

Another fall. Who was shooting in the dark? Begg could think of only two men. Swiftly his hand went to his pocket – and found it empty. Following his own rules, he had left his automatic in the car.

The whole club was now in uproar. Half the clientele was armed and Begg knew there was a real danger of being caught in aimless crossfire. He overturned their table, pushing Yvette behind it as wine, glasses and plates smashed to the floor. Cautiously he switched on his slender torch, the thin beam of bright light seeking the source of the problem. The other diners he spotted were quite as bewildered as he was. Keeping to whatever cover he had, Begg took Yvette's hand and made his way towards the kitchens where he knew the fuse boxes would be. He pushed through the milling customers and waiters to get to the kitchens, his free hand still grasping Yvette's.

"Here!" he showed her the box and a lever which had been turned from ON to OFF. "There's our answer. Now let's try to see who switched them off."

Rapidly, the detectives returned to the main room. They found the place almost deserted. Few customers of French Tony's could afford to be mixed up in any violence not of their own initiation. It was astonishing how swiftly they could 'disappear'. A number of waiters were gathering around two men who lay on the floor.

"Let us through, please! I'm a doctor." Begg told the truth. He was a qualified M.D., though he did not practice. The prone man was a small, foreign-looking individual whose long fingers were curled around a dangerous looking 'cane knife' or *machete* of the kind used in the jungles of South America and the West Indies. His aquiline features were unusually pale, with greasy hair swept back. He wore a reasonably expensive suit and a shirt of good quality. Kneeling beside the corpse and automatically feeling for a pulse, Begg saw at once that the man could not have lived. He had two bullet holes – one between the eyes and another through the heart. Yet he was scarcely bleeding. Frowning, Begg inspected the face. Surely he had seen it somewhere before.

Looking beyond him, Begg checked over another, smaller figure lying nearby. Plump, rotund, bald and clean-shaven this man, too, was dead. And familiar. Another *macheté* had dropped from his hand. The third shot had taken him, also, straight between the eyes. His weapon lay a short distance from where he had fallen. Begg's opinion was confirmed. Only three men were good enough with the small pistol to snap such shots. One was himself, another was Hoxton Ryman. The last was Monsieur Zenith. It appeared that the shot men had attacked while he and Yvette were absorbed in their dance. A third must have switched off the electrics and disappeared when the customers fled. Both dead men were obviously of European origin. By their clothes and appearance, they had lived by a skilled trade. Why would such obvious Continentals be carrying long, terrible knives found chiefly in the cane fields and jungles of tropical America?

"The extraordinary thing is that at least two of those shots were fired in pitch darkness," mused Begg, standing up.

But Zenith, the only man known to possess uncanny accuracy when firing by sound alone with the notoriously inaccurate 'derringer' type of pistol and a .38 at that, was nowhere to be seen. Begg looked everywhere around him. Ryman, Vespa and Molly Dent had also disappeared with most of the other diners!

As one, the two detectives ran up the stairs and into the street just in time to see a Daimler limousine, driven by a handsome Japanese, disappear in the direction of central London, leaving the chain across the entrance unsecured.

Although they turned towards their car, Begg and Yvette felt no compunction to follow. They knew from old experience that Zenith would be impossible to track now he had such a good start. Also two constables had arrived and were asking the remaining guests not to leave.

"We all forget our road manners after we've shot two men dead and not stopped to argue 'self-defence'." The sarcastic voice came from behind them. Turning, they recognised the familiar, stolid figure of their old friend from Scotland Yard C.I.D., Detective Inspector Coutts. His bowler hat clamped firmly on his massive head, his horrible pipe blowing black smoke into the cold night air, he bent to replace the chain in its proper place.

"Well, well, well. What d'you think happened down there, Begg?" Gravely, Coutts bowed to Yvette, raising his bowler. "Ma'am."

She was the first to speak, smiling. "Good evening, Inspector. What brings you to French Tony's? Their beef wellington is especially good tonight." Yvette was at her prettiest and most flattering.

"Ah, mam'selle, if only I had a chance to sit down to a decent dinner! But I didn't come for the cuisine. We were following two very suspicious customers."

Begg's smile was thin. "Were they carrying 'jungle knives' and was one of them a dead ringer for that well-known master-forger Peter Hess?"

Coutts was clearly impressed. There was something like a grin on his red, rotund face as he replied. "That would be breaking regulations if I was to tell you." He winked and, apologizing, asked them to wait while he stepped in to the club.

Five minutes later Coutts came back up, his breath steaming in the late October gloom. He clapped his gloved hands together to warm them. "Well, Begg, I won't say you were wrong about Hess. Looked as if he'd been ill to me. He was busted out of the Scrubs not two months ago. Complete mystery how. The other dead man could have been a colleague of his. Name's Alphonse LeGris, known as the 'Improver'. A French doctor. Clever chap. Specialised in plastic surgery. Not just subtle alterations to faces, but he could graft another man's fingerprints onto your hands if you so desired. Struck off a few years back for helping alter the appearance of Jacques Villeneuve, the famous embezzler. He was also 'sprung' from gaol recently, equally mysteriously. No connection between 'em. They had never met. Not even been in the same prison together. But the really funny thing about them, Begg —"

"Was that they weren't given to violence, certainly not murder. They depended on their skills for a living. Nothing could have persuaded either man to arm wrestle, let alone attack some chap with some kind of cleaver. What did they have against one of French Tony's customers, I wonder?"

"They were probably expected, the way the killer responded. But it was self-defence, I suppose."

"From what I've gathered someone put out the lights and they came in through a service door. Headed straight for where Ryman and Zenith were sitting with their lady friends and were shot before they could carry out their mission."

"And did you notice their eyes, the strange pallor of their skin?" Yvette asked, reminding the men that she was a good detective, too. "Their clothing, though a little the worse for wear, was of fine quality. Tailored suits. Not the sort of outfits you usually wear to commit a bloody murder."

"Quite so," agreed Coutts admiringly. "Well, as I'm sure you've both guessed, we followed those two to Tony's. We're not here by coincidence. And it's not the only funny thing going on in London tonight. If this is London. Are we still in London?"

"Just," said Begg dryly. "So what else is going on, Coutts?"

"How about a raw fowl being found in Hyde Park and all sorts of odd ciphers and words cut into trees or daubed on walls in the vicinity? Maybe even human torture? That pair was involved. Gruesome stuff but not exactly murder. We followed them from the park to here..." There was a strange look in his eyes as he uttered this phrase. "They can't scare an old-fashioned London copper like yours truly." He frowned as he winked at Begg. "Who was that in the posh motor car? Who I think it was?"

Begg smiled. "If you think it was Zenith – "

"I'd be right, eh?. And his pals Ryman, Vespa and Molly Dent, if I'm not mistaken," jerked Coutts, "all left at the same time. "But it was Zenith doing the shooting, right?"

"Ryman, too, would be my guess," Begg agreed. "And you're right, too, about it being self-defence. That pair came out of nowhere. It felt spooky. Almost supernatural."

Coutts nodded slowly. "Not a spontaneous act. Any attempted murder tonight was planned. I wonder what Hess and LeGris had against our friends. This isn't a gangland war, though someone might hope we mistake it for one. Dead chickens. Blood. Torture. Some sort of Black Mass. Here. I copied a few of the symbols we found in Hyde Park." Coutts took a regulation notebook from the pocket of his crumpled suit. "What do you make of them?"

Begg studied the drawings and handed the book to Yvette. "I could be wrong, but those symbols remind me of some I've seen in the Caribbean."

"You recognise them?"

"I think so. Especially the man in the top hat. And the crowing black cockerels. The 'Queen of the Night'. They're associated with Hayti. To be specific, a Voodoo cult belonging extensively to that island republic," said Begg. "But I think you know as much already. What's this about orgiastic rituals in the park?"

"We've been finding the signs there for a week or so and I've had men watching, just in case. And we've been keeping an eye on sailors from South America and the Caribbean. One of our chaps has studied the religions and cults imported and adapted from Africa. He recognized the symbols and the other signs of some sort of black magic ritual. There's some suggestion of human sacrifice, too. Who would have thought to see such things going on in the twentieth century!" Coutts shook his head wonderingly.

Begg ignored this. He had seen too much and too many aspects of mankind to be surprised. What he did want to know, however, was why the dead men had been attacking Zenith or the others. "There's a great deal that doesn't meet the eye in this business," he said softly as he escorted Mlle Yvette back to the Silver Spectre. He called back over his shoulder. "Goodnight, Coutts. And good luck!"

Coutts's eyes widened. "You're not going to help us?"

"You seem to have the business under control," Begg said blithely. He opened the door for Yvette. "One thing you could do, though, if you wouldn't mind."

"What's that?"

"Be a good chap and take the chain off the hook, would you? It's late and it's time I got this young woman home before I'm in trouble with her uncle."

Shaking his head resignedly, Coutts moved to comply.

"Oh, there is one thing which might interest you, Coutts, concerning the two shot men."

"What's that?" With an expression of mock distaste, Coutts stopped, the chain in his hand.

Begg poked his head out of the window as he drove slowly past. "Your forensics people will confirm it, I'm sure. Those two were dead long before they were shot here." With a wave he let out the clutch and disappeared in the direction of the city, leaving a baffled Detective Inspector scratching his head and pondering the meaning of Begg's last, cryptic remark.

CHAPTER TWO
A Quiet Sunday Morning in Baker Street

NEXT MORNING WAS Sunday. Mrs Hardnutt sang to herself downstairs and periodically handed trays or plates to Yvette and Winker who were helping her as much as she allowed, while upstairs Seaton Begg sat beside the fire, puffing on his ancient briar, looking through the news and thinking over the events of the previous evening. Something had been nagging at his brain since he had got up and even when Yvette came in with fresh bread from the nearby French baker he had hardly said a word. Eventually, he flung the last of the British and foreign papers aside and beaming as only the smell of freshly fried bacon and eggs could make him beam, joined the others at the table while Stone the bloodhound stared longingly from the hearthrug.

Begg took part in the familiar small talk, though it was clear he was a little distracted. As usual, they spoke only of light, amusing matters and never breathed a word about their cases. It had become convenient for the two detectives to share office facilities and so they did not discuss business in what leisure time they had.

The apartments were no longer in Baker Street, which now housed an expanded set of offices, but nearby, just a few streets away.[1] After breakfast, Begg announced he intended to take Stone out for a short stroll and call in at the office where he wanted to have a quick glance through some of their reference books.

"You've been brooding about that affair all night," complained Yvette. "Has no one told you that Sunday is a day of rest?"

Begg smiled. "I promise I'll be back in time for our concert on the wireless." He attached Stone's leash to the dog's collar, took a

---

[1] Although there are several theories concerning the location of 'Begg's' apartments, it is agreed that they were only a short walk from his consulting rooms.

hat down from the rack and sauntered out into the cool, sharp morning air.

Once he arrived at the office, Begg soon lost himself in the famous Index and completely forgot the time until he heard the doorbell ring downstairs. Feeling a little guilty and assuming Yvette had not brought her keys, knowing Minnie Jones, their receptionist didn't work on Sunday, Begg went down to open the door. He found not the slender beauty of Mlle Yvette but the stolid form complete with bowler hat and a pipe quite as foul as Begg's own, of Detective Inspector Coutts of Scotland Yard.

Begg was a little surprised, "What on earth can be so important that you of all people, Coutts, can be dragged from your family Sunday and forced to interrupt mine. I thought we had a pact, old man."

Coutts went past Begg and began to climb the stairs to the main consulting room. When he arrived he plumped himself down in an armchair and sighed like the Royal Scot drawing in to King's Cross. "Again, I apologise for busting in on your day of rest, Begg, but this really couldn't wait. I knew you wouldn't be in church and I guessed you might be here."

Seating himself in the chair opposite, Begg made a quick telephone call to a rather unhappy Yvette and, lighting his own pipe, sat back.

Coutts reddened a little before clearing his throat. "My sooper was brought out of *his* pew this morning and consequently was on the phone to me to deal with it."

"Spit it out, old man," Begg was almost smiling at his old friend's discomfort. "Is it about those two shootings last night?"

"How did you know? Oh, I suppose you know everything! Ha! Well, yes. It's about the victims or whatever you choose to call 'em. I don't know how you knew, but it's true the bullets didn't kill them. Or at least, weren't the cause of death. Our pathologist suggested they had been dead for hours, even days, before they were shot. Yet French Tony and his waiters swear they were alive when they appeared at the club like a couple of avenging angels. They just materialized, apparently, shortly before the lights went out. We think they had a woman accomplice who dealt with the lights. You saw nothing?"

"I was dancing."

Coutts drew a deep breath. "Well, you might as well know –"

"Those walking dead men walked again?" Begg looked up quizzically. "They slid off their slabs and strolled out into the night just like that!"

Coutts shook his head and stared at his boots with a sad, contemplative air. "Not quite, Begg. But close. They disappeared from the morgue. A young constable dashed out to look for them, but they'd vanished. The only witness was an old drunkard who swore he saw them walk into the water and climb into a motor launch which disappeared upriver. If you are so dashed prescient, why couldn't you have known that would happen last night?"

"Well, I guessed evidence like that would prove embarrassing and someone decided to recover it! But how could I interfere when the case was already a police matter?"

"Hmph, hasn't stopped you in the past." Coutts was now a rather alarming shade of puce. "In that case, I officially ask for your – um – consulting services…"

"If you're sure I can help." Begg smiled his amusement at his old friend's discomfort. He sprang up and left the room, returning after a moment with a slim, leather-bound volume Coutts recognized as one of Begg's learned monographs.

Taking the book, Coutts read the spine. "*Some Recently Added Elements to Caribbean Quasi-religious Cults, Notably Haytian Voodoo.* Voodoo? I never suspected you of all people of dabbling in that kind of mumbo-jumbo! Or that you were a member of the Royal Society!"

"I assure you, Coutts, the Voodoo religion is no mere mumbo-jumbo and is no less spiritually satisfying than any other Faith. Genuine Voodoo believers are chiefly Catholic and venerate Christ and the Bible quite as much as your own Welsh Baptist cousins,"

"Well, you know a great deal more about that sort of thing than I might. But the fact remains, Begg, our two murder victims went missing from the morgue at Richmond Central at around 3am this morning. Possibly helped by members of the same gang. I have one very jittery young constable who found them gone, without quite realizing what it was he missed."

"And what was that?" Begg asked mildly, selecting a fresh pipe from the rack on his desk.

"I told you. He thought they walked. On their own two feet. Out of the morgue and out towards the river. By the time we got some men there they'd vanished. Not a trace! Our only witness, an old drunkard, had them walking into the water to a waiting motor boat which went on up the river towards Chiswick."

"Hardly worth interrupting a chap's day off," grumbled Begg, his brows drawn together in thought. "Didn't I tell you what was involved?"

"Nothing specific. You hinted at something. So I thought..."

Begg nodded. "I seem to have made a rod for my own back, Very well, Coutts. Let's start with the obvious people. Dr Ryman and Miss Dent?"

Coutts consulted his notes. "Back at Yarn Abbey, Kent. As Professor Butterworth and his niece. When asked, said they were certainly at French Tony's last night but that the lights must have gone out after they left. No proof to the contrary. Zenith, of course, cannot be found. Signorina Vespa della Vulpa was at the Savoy last night. We got to her just as she was leaving to catch the midnight boat train to Paris. She denied all knowledge of Zenith, naturally, except as a man with whom she might have danced at French Tony's. There was nothing we could hold her for since she, too, denied seeing anything."

"Paris, eh?" Begg was still deep in thought. "Ryman's favourite Continental city."

"What's that mean?"

"Maybe nothing at all. But it is always possible that if Ryman is involved then one of his female partners in crime is also an element of our pattern. Maybe Vespa, though I didn't see them together last night. And possibly it's Marie Leveaux of Hayti – the infamous 'Voodoo queen' who's been mixed up in all kinds of trouble from Nicaragua to New Orleans and Port au Prince to Port o' Spain. She

64

claims to desire a black takeover of the islands and has her eye on large parts of South and Central America – wherever black people exist in sufficient numbers. She claims to challenge Britain's presence in Africa, playing on the frustrations of dissidents in the British, American and French colonies. Actually she only serves her own interests."

"Why would she be in Europe? She has no interests here, surely?"

"Only if there is some financial gain for her. She has followers everywhere, especially in sea-ports like New York, New Orleans, Rotterdam, London, Liverpool, Marseilles, Spain, Casablanca, Tunis, Tripoli or any other part of the Dark Continent. Her plans are complex and long-term. She has amongst her followers some skilful Voodoo priests and priestesses. Sometimes the women pretend to be her, to make it seem she's everywhere at the same time. They can achieve effects which baffle the most experienced and intelligent investigators. She, however, uses drugs to induce specific conditions in the worshippers of her particular cult."

"Surely you don't think those men last night were really – what d'you call 'em – zanies or something?"

"Those are circus clowns, Coutts. I think the word you're looking for is *zombis*."

"That's it!" Coutts rubbed his big chin. "Totally fantastic."

"Oh, certainly, if you're talking about a film," said Begg, "but not if you're discussing the extraordinary powers of suggestion that woman possesses. She's the finest hypnotist alive. And she can mesmerise crowds even better than Vespa's countryman Prime Minister Mussolini. She's the real thing, all right, Coutts, whatever the 'real thing' is, and anyone would be a fool to underestimate her. Winker and I have witnessed some astonishing sights in the Caribbean, believe me."

"Yet, if those two *were* her servants, she can't be all-powerful or Zenith – if it were Zenith – couldn't have shot them. And they were shot. Forensics were clear about that. You say they were some sort of 'walking dead' monsters! If she could bring them back to life from a distance and make them walk down to the Thames into a waiting boat, I'll eat – " He exchanged a wry glance with Begg – "my Sunday lunch!"

"I'm not suggesting she uses what we think of as magic to control her people," gritted Begg evenly, "for she knows more about tropical medicines and herbs than anyone alive, but I am perfectly prepared to accept she has powers beyond our ken. If I did not, I should be a fool. Very well, Coutts, leave it with me. It's very likely I will be stretching my own beliefs with this problem. We must trust to our instincts if we are to succeed in cracking the case. My guess is that we shall all learn something before it's over. And I can only hope we all survive in one piece. If Marie LeVeaux is involved, I should warn you that she can be a vicious, cold-blooded opponent who is scared of no one and stops at nothing to achieve her ends."

Coutts heaved his body from his armchair and put his hat back on his head. "Be assured, Begg, if such a woman is at large in London, she won't escape from us."

Begg rose to show his friend out. "I certainly hope you're right, Coutts."

Soon after the policeman had left   Begg locked up the offices and made his thoughtful way back to his flat where Winker and Yvette were waiting eagerly to hear what had transpired.

CHAPTER THREE
At Yarn Abbey

DR HOXTON RYMAN stared broodingly into the great blaze of logs settling in the fireplace of the main hall at Yarn Abbey, the old Kent manor he and Molly Dent used under their pseudonyms of Professor Alec Butterworth and his niece Miss Appleby. He frowned as he picked up the poker and stirred the logs. The events of Saturday evening were still on his mind. For quite a while he had been prepared, as Alec Butterworth, to continue pursuing the research which had made his name – or actually his pseudonym – synonymous in the medical and academic communities with scientific progress. Butterworth was revered for relieving the suffering of large parts of the world's population. And while he continued to do so, the authorities were prepared to grant him an amnesty for his many crimes. "Well, Molly? Do you still think I was wrong to trust her?"

Molly Dent had become his most daring partner, loving him uncritically, whatever he chose to do. She raised one slim, enquiring eyebrow. "You think Marie Levaux was behind last night's attack?"

"She must suspect us of betraying her."

"Yet you have worked so hard to produce what she wants. Day and night, you've been in the laboratory until – until you achieved what others would deem impossible!"

"Quite so. As she asked, I arranged a meeting between herself and her 'customers'. Yet, as soon as she had what she wanted, those ghouls turned up at Tony's with murder in mind. Lord knows what they would have done if they hadn't been stopped. And on the very night Begg was there, too! Well, he can sniff around all he likes, I haven't really broken our agreement. You can be sure I would not. Thanks to our unstable friend! I must suppose we are not in partnership any more. I did everything she asked, however reluctantly, and got what we wanted. Why I didn't anticipate that attack, I don't know."

"Probably because you had not allowed for how crazy she is. She's horribly jealous of any other woman, Hoxton. It wasn't in her self-interest to break our agreement. But I have to tell you, I would rather forget all about it than have this go on. Even if it means my – my –" And her eyes filled suddenly with tears.

Ryman nodded slowly. "I've been too distracted with our other problems to worry about the risks... That's why I didn't see this coming, I guess."

"Could she have found a new partner? Zenith –?"

"Zenith fired two of the shots that brought the first man down. Why would he do that?   I know Marie. She regards her people as her property, If Zenith killed one of 'her' people, she will hold that against him. His life is doubtless now in danger. But last night she wanted to kill me. I have done all she asked and I received what she promised. I achieved what I so desperately desired. You know that better than anyone. That was our deal. But then she wanted to make me work for her permanently and I couldn't do that. I tell you, Molly, if she comes after me again, I will kill her. I mean it. Our deal is done. I want no more to do with her. And so she takes offence and strikes out! I understand how my decision galls her. Now *I* must die, it seems. Probably because I resisted her charms the other night. Se no doubt perceives that as an insult. Otherwise I have served my turn. Maybe she doesn't trust me not to pass on the secret of my synthesis. My guess is that she has set her sights on a more agreeable scientist or she thinks that the quantity I distilled for her will last indefinitely. Well, she is wrong there."

Molly shook her head sadly. She knew why Ryman had compromised and taken such considerable risks. It pained her to see him in this position. "Since we don't know if those goons were trying to get us, I suppose we must wait for her to try again."

"That depends how many 'customers' she wants to create. You saw who those two were. Doubtless they also refused to go on doing her rotten work. She'll find others. She's greedy and insanely proud."

"Indeed." With a sigh Molly returned her attention to the sampler on which she was working. "And Vespa?"

"Could be Marie's new partner. You know how mercurial she is. Vespa lives in Paris and the only other man who comes close to matching my work is in Paris. For all I know he pipped me to the post as far as learning how to produce quantity goes."

"And that would explain Zenith's involvement?"

"Possibly." He frowned into the fire. "Unlikely, again. If he thought the matter over, he would realize that I am a better partner than Marie. I could use him as an ally. It might be wise to call a conference of war and suggest Vespa and Zenith join us. Zenith could operate from Paris and our parole would not be compromised. But only Marie has the power of hypnosis and Voodoo. Sadly, of course, she can never be really trusted. Her emotions rule her head at crucial times."

Ryman straightened up, frowning. "I'll call a conference tomorrow if I can. Marie, Vespa and Zenith. Here will do."

Molly Dent sighed. Her female instincts told her there was more going on than either of them realized. She wished with all her heart that Ryman had not taken up with the Voodoo Queen again. She knew why and it made her love him all the more. But she had guessed it meant trouble from the start. She shivered as if an icy current of air had passed through the room.

"I'm going down to the lab," Ryman said. "Most of the large animals recovered. They can be sent back or released into the wild. I'd like to start closing it up. A couple more weeks should do it. Then maybe we should go away for a month or two until this whole business has died down?"

"I would love that," said Molly. "I have to say I preferred life before that woman came into it." She lifted her hand to silence him. "I understand why you have done what you have done, however."

Although he did not voice his agreement, he was inclined to wish his feelings had not got the better of him. As Professor Butterworth and his niece, they had enjoyed an existence which did not involve fear of the law and neither were their lives threatened by the living dead. Now, he guessed, that secure life was over. They would have to begin again, forever on the run, forever looking over their shoulders. Yet, he had to admit, he still considered it worth all he was going through. If only there had been some other way!

CHAPTER FOUR
A strange undertaking.

ALTHOUGH THEY SHARED an address and office facilities, Mr Seaton Begg and Mlle Yvette Bouvier rarely shared clients. They kept their business lives rigorously apart to ensure that client-privilege was never compromised. The Baker Street building had been carefully modified and numbered so that no client of Begg's or Mlle Bouvier should ever visit the wrong detective. Rarely was there any confusion. They even went to work by different routes.

On the following Monday morning, however, Yvette was to receive something of a shock. As she walked along Baker Street enjoying the pleasures of a bright autumn morning, a well-dressed, balding man, a little dishevelled, in early middle-age ran up behind her, clutching at her sleeve. "Mademoiselle Bouvier, please! I am desperate. Can you help me?"

"I'm so sorry. I've no change!"

"Oh, I'll pay you anything you want. Everything I have. It's not for me but for my family – my family name."

She paused only a few steps from the office. "What?"

He stood, red-faced and panting before her, like a worried spaniel. "My name is Jarvis, ma'am. I need your help, the help of your firm – professionally. I recognise you from the picture papers. You are more beautiful in the – in person." He blushed and stammered. "Will you hear me out? Then, if you ask me to leave, I shall."

Yvette enjoyed such flattery but it rarely clouded her judgement. Now she saw in the man's eyes a strange bafflement mixed with fear. He was in great distress.

"Very well, Mr Jarvis. We'll go into the office, shall we?" She led him into her own suite which had already been opened by her assistant Minnie. Telling the girl to hold any calls, she said to him: "I must point out, however, that if you are not entirely frank with me I shall be unable to accept your case." Taking off her coat she indicated a chair. He sat down. Then she went to her own seat and opened her notebook.

"Well, Mr Jarvis, the stage is all yours." Her voice was now polite, reassuring, professional. She could not help feeling sympathetic. His hair was unbrushed, his clothes untidy, yet she could tell by the condition of his nails and suit that this was a man who usually took care of his appearance.

"Thank you, mademoiselle. Well, I hardly believe it myself, I suppose, or I wouldn't be here. You probably won't believe me, either, but at least you've dealt with some queer cases, if the newspapers and periodicals are right."

"They all sensationalise humdrum reality." She smiled. "Please continue, Mr Jarvis."

He brushed back the hair around his ears and made an effort to collect himself. "You might have heard of my firm, Miss Bouvier. Jarvis Sons and Jarvis. We are funeral directors in Mayfair. Indeed, we are the only firm of funeral directors in Mayfair. We have a very select list of clients, as you can imagine. We have buried more than one titled head."

"I am sure, Mr Jarvis." Yvette made a note. "Please go on.

Jarvis described how, in the past week, they were making arrangements for three 'clients', the Earl of Morn, Mr Arthur Price, 'an unmarried young Honourable', and a retired JP, Sir Gordon Ogg. "All of them rather tragic cases, I have to say. Relatively young men in their prime."

"How did they die?" she asked, continuing to make notes.

"That's the first strange thing, mademoiselle. All were in reasonable health. All died from natural causes."

"Which were?"

"It was believed they died of heart attacks."

"No foul play suspected?"

"Good heavens, no! Tragic circumstances, most certainly, but we have had younger clients in the past who died of similar causes. In the midst of life, Mlle Bouvier..."

"Indeed." She signed for him to continue. "But you have reason, perhaps, to think there were suspicious circumstances to their deaths?"

"Oh, not at all! Everyone involved is far above suspicion. We were called, of course, on the recommendation of doctors whose clients have used our services before. Everything was in order, including the death certificates. We have, I should emphasise, an unsullied reputation. We have been established in Burlington Row, our present address, since 1778. We prepared the Duke of Wellington, for instance, although we did not of course arrange the

71

lying in state or – ahem – the plot. Since then, the list has been a distinguished one."

"I'm sure. Then —?"

"It is, I fear, what happened *after* they came to us for preparation."

"Afterwards?"

"Yes,ma'am. They disappeared from our premises as we were due to prepare them for the final stages of their – um – journey."

"Their corpses were *stolen*?"

"Not on the face of it." Mr Jarvis again showed considerable distress. "It seems they climbed down from our preparation tables under their own volition and walked out of our premises at some time in the night of Saturday and Sunday last."

"*Walked*, Mr Jarvis? But you said they —"

"Were dead. Precisely, ma'am. With death certificates from Doctors Burrowes and Benway. All absolutely above board."

"Where did they go when they left – um – Burlington Row?"

"That's the problem, mademoiselle. We don't know. They did not return to their homes, one of which is quite nearby in Albemarle Street. The only reason we know they walked out of the preparation rooms was on the evidence of our own nightwatchman, whom we employ to guard the various expensive substances involved in our work. You would be surprised, for instance, what some would pay for a few ounces of frankincense."

The man was both frightened and anxious. Yvette realised his entire living was at stake. He was, at least in his own view, unquestionably facing ruin. That was why he had lost no time in coming to see her, the only other consulting detective in London's West End. He admitted quite openly that he had thought of approaching Seaton Begg but had decided in the end that a woman might give him a sympathetic ear. Besides, he had spotted her as he approached the office and was convinced Fate had directed him.

"I'm so sorry not to be as calm as I usually am, Miss Bouvier." His voice shook as he spoke. "But I have to tell you that my nerves are shattered and that I face ruin – absolute ruin – if this business cannot be resolved quickly and discreetly! One does not

72

lose clients in my profession. As it is, I am not at all sure the day can be saved, even if the mystery is solved!

"Anyone of prominence in our part of town, it's safe to say – *was* safe to say, I suppose, now – knew that their beloved relatives and friends were in the best possible hands, both professional and discrete, when they entrusted us with the last remains of their dear ones. Our funerals are dignified and proceed with the smoothest possible regularity, allowing for every eventuality and ensuring that nothing can occur which threatens the peace of mind of our clients. That is, miss, until last Saturday night. Mr Archibald, the nightwatchman, actually saw them leave Burlington Row. He followed them, believing at first that he was probably dreaming, and told me he saw them all three get into a big car – perhaps a taxi – which drove off towards the river."

With her slim silver propelling pencil Yvette made notes, asking him to spell proper names and fill in a little of the men's backgrounds, including any medical history they might have. Mr Arthur Price, it emerged, had died of a stroke at the relatively young age of 50. Iain St Claire, seventh Earl of Morn, in his 55th year, had been an active sportsman and like the others had also died of a stroke. The youngest was Sir Gordon Ogg, a Justice of the Peace. Their funerals were all due to be held at the church of Saint James, Piccadilly, one on the coming Thursday and the other two on the following Monday. All three, it appeared, had led the active, outdoor lives of men of their class.

Mlle Yvette could not help thinking of the case on which Seaton Begg was currently working with Inspector Coutts. Was it a coincidence? Typically, she risked, as it were, a shot in the dark.

"Have you ever heard of *zombis*, Mr Jarvis?"

"*Zombis!* Did you say *zombis*, ma'am." Mr Jarvis was now very pale. To her own surprise, Yvette saw that her question had struck home.

"I did, Mr Jarvis." She leaned forward, her lovely eyes widening as she peered into his. "A silly notion, of course and I suppose I should apologise for mentioning the phenomenon. Fiction, I know..."

"Ah!" He seemed relieved.

"But you've heard the term?"

"In the past," he said. "Long ago." He looked at her frankly. "I'm not at all superstitious, you understand, but I spent a few years out in Jamaica and the Caribbean, where the firm has a branch. We provide a service for people of quality whose own affairs take them to that part of the world. We were based in Bermuda but drew clients from all over the Americas. That's where I heard the stories. *Zombis!* Oh, dear me!" He attempted a rather ghastly smile.

"I was merely making an association, Mr Jarvis." She offered him a searching glance.

"Of course, mademoiselle."

"Yet you almost took me seriously, if I'm not mistaken!" Mlle Yvette's nose for the truth was telling her something she did not yet quite understand. "You'll forgive me if I pursue the subject? I, too, have spent time in the Caribbean islands. Do you fear the Living Dead of the Voodoo world, Mr Jarvis?"

"Of course not, ma'am. I should hardly be in this profession if I did! But I did see things – and hear of more – which rather challenged one's notions of normality. Perfectly rationally explained, no doubt. I saw things out there which rather defeat one's normal upbringing. I did not give in to it but I must admit I came close on occasions. Never so far as to 'go native', of course. And we talked of field hands, not respectable Londoners! A bit blood-curdling, but hardly making sense to a man of my upbringing. I was young and curious..."

"You sound as if you actually attended a local ceremony!"

He looked up suddenly, studying her face as if weighing her words and his own reply. Then he shrugged and sighed. "I went twice, when we were on a trip to Cuba, myself and a young man called Prentice. And twice Baron Samedi singled me out. I danced – oh, how I danced. It was, I will admit, exhilarating, but that was all."

"He singled you out?" She found that her curiosity was stronger than she had thought.

"As a Chosen One! The locals were rather impressed. It's complete nonsense. I resisted, but it proved harder than I had judged it would and after that it grew too unpleasant. I begged my father to send someone else out and to bring me home. If I seem frightened, ma'am, it could be I was followed back here by people who had it in for me. All mumbo jumbo, of course. I even wondered once if perhaps I carried the smell of death about my person!"

When Yvette looked up next she had a look of resolution in her lovely indigo eyes. "Mr Jarvis, when you came here, I said I would only take your case if you were entirely frank with me. Yet you are still holding something back. Was there a woman involved?"

Mr Jarvis almost started from his chair, "How did you —? I mean, how could you possibly make such an assumption?" Then he sank back, burying his head in his hands, "Yes, Yes. And don't think I'm not ashamed. I should never have – I mean, I thought it was all over. She was so beautiful. And she carried herself like a queen. Well, she was a queen, of sorts. How many men could resist such exotic beauty?" He leaned forward across the desk. "I mean no insult to other beautiful women, ma'am, but she had all the allure of Lilith. She made my heart beat faster. My head was full of the sound of that constant drumming. A chap got me out of there before I did something I would thoroughly regret. That's why I was sent back. She wanted me to steal – steal from my own people. I resisted. She grew more persuasive but thankfully my father had wind of it and I was recalled. Even on the ship home I still heard that terrible drumming in my head. Sometimes, even now, I sometimes wake up in the middle of the night hearing it. *Bomba! Bomba! Bomba!*" He sank back with his head in his hands. "Oh, I could hardly keep my sanity! She was so fiendishly desirable!"

"You believe this woman followed you to England?"

"Sometimes. In the dead of night. At other times I think I see her face in a passing car or hear her voice in a crowd."

"And you believe she is bringing your – your clients – back to life and that now – now they are —?"

"If she is here in London, ma'amselle, those poor people could by now be her slaves. Living dead men who will perform any crime – any crime – if she so orders! I don't know how you guessed, Mlle Yvette, but if it is she, if there's no other explanation, she must be found and she must be stopped!"

Yvette did not betray her own skepticism of Jarvis's story but the case itself was beginning to fascinate her. So, under her usual terms, she told Jarvis that she would look into the case and hoped to reassure him that no mumbo jumbo was being practiced in the heart of Mayfair!

When the still pale Jarvis had left, Yvette leaned back in her chair, a delicate little finger raised to her pretty chin. Her keen eyes were burning with intelligence as she set her mind to contemplating the case. Begg had told her little of Coutts's request and she wondered now if there were any point to bringing him in. She knew how busy he was and believed he would scoff at a tale involving *zombis* and their queen. So she decided at least to begin her investigation without telling him about it. Perhaps later...

CHAPTER FIVE
Incident on the Calais-Paris Express

M.ZENITH, THE Albino, studied his reflection in the mirror of his Pullman suite as the Calais-Paris express moaned and swayed her way across the moonlit French countryside. The melancholy, which was always in his eyes, disappeared for a moment as he spoke with self-mocking irony.

"As usual, Oyami, you have done well."

"M'sieu is gracious." Behind him his Japanese valet put the finishing touches to his perfect evening dress. Earlier, on the boat, Oyami had prepared his master's opium, all with the connivance of men who would lay down their lives for Zenith, who owed him more than they could repay. That was why, in recent years as his reputation grew, he had been able to come and go freely in the world, almost at will. Not that he had ever knowingly bribed a man nor given him a favour with any thought of repayment.

With a languorous movement of his hand, Zenith added his silk hat and picked up his ebony evening cane, ready to partake of the meal his own chefs were preparing in the Pullman's kitchens. He sighed as his servant opened the door on to the corridor, revealing the nightscape of France flashing by outside.

For a second the Albino paused, catching sight of his own reflection, a night animal in its natural environment, the milk white skin, the strange, crimson eyes, like two glittering rubies, the slender, muscular build, the sleek appearance – he might have been a wild mountain cat on the prowl for prey. With a soft grunt of dissatisfaction, he walked along the corridor, the spring in his step only serving to emphasise the impression of controlled power which he exuded from every pore. Zenith only knew something like happiness when he was in action, risking his life in some daring theft or quixotic adventure involving a lady.

Reaching the opulent dining car and removing his hat, Zenith let the steward open the door for him and entered, taking his place at a table set for two. The time was unusual for breakfast and the meal itself was also unusual.

There were only two other passengers in the carriage: well-to-do ladies no longer in their first youth, also there for an early breakfast. Deep in conversation, they hardly noticed the Albino's entrance as he gave an order for two aperitifs, rising as his guest entered the carriage and offering a dignified greeting. Vespa della Vulpa seemed to float along the aisle, presenting her gorgeous, beringed hand for him to kiss. "Good morning, my dear count."

He bowed. "I no longer possess a title or a name," he said gently as he straightened. "You know better than any, why I choose the nom de guerre of Zenith."

She acknowledged this as she took her seat. "Forgive me. I was recalling happier times, when we both had countries we could call our own." She flicked her napkin to her lap. "I see you have not forgotten what I like to drink."

He acknowledged this. "I hope you are equally happy with my chef's choices."

In a moment the waiter brought her favourite foie gras. She was delighted, especially after she had taken her first bite of the delicacy. They spoke little during this course, occasionally glancing out of the window as the shadowy countryside flashed by. Then, suddenly, Zenith was alert. He had seen something in the reflective glass and every nerve was signalling danger. Yet he continued to eat as if he were the most relaxed diner in the world. Only his eyes took in what was happening. Moments later, he put down his knife and fork and murmured an apology. "A moment."

Rising with studied insouciance, the Albino stepped swiftly to the communicating door, his ebony stick held casually in his left hand. He had seen reflected in the glass of the opposite window that at least two figures were on the roof of the speeding train. They were moving towards the gap separating one carriage from another!

Losing no time, Zenith let down the window in the corridor. Without hesitating he swung his lithe body through the opening just as a face peered over the lip of the roof. That face might have given any other man pause. It was oddly non-reflective. Even the eyes looked like those of a long-caught fish. His skin, as white as Zenith's own, had a repulsive, pasty quality.

Zenith had seen eyes and skin like that before. But what surprised him was that he also recognised with a shock the man's identity! Unmistakeably, he was a petty crook called Gentleman Jordan whom Zenith himself had sometimes employed. They had probably been on the train since Victoria. But now Gentleman Jordan was filled with whatever strange vitality was being used in the creation of these zombis. His eyes rolled in his head as he aimed a clumsy blow at the Albino.

Holding the hand-rail beside the window Zenith leaned out and jabbed swiftly with his cane, driving the ferule hard into the man's left eye. Rearing back, the creature silently withdrew. A moment later a long jungle knife came out of the darkness and would have descended on the Albino's head were he still there. But he was already out of the window, swinging around until he could clutch at the ladder running up the outside of his own carriage.

Ascending rapidly, Zenith reached the swaying roof as, snarling, his would-be attacker again came at him out of the darkness. The wound to his eye was apparently unnoticed, though clearly he had been blinded. The ebony stick lashed out once more, chopping at the man's legs just below the knees. He wobbled for a moment, his macheté windmilling as he tried to regain his balance. But it was impossible. With a grunt he fell backwards, his body disappearing into the darkness.

Straightening, Zenith saw three others advancing towards him. All had the same glassy eyes and white, dead skin. He knew what they were and he knew who had sent them. Last night he had shot one and let Ryman take the other. Now he had no ally and no chance to use his little two-shot .38. He ducked another wide swing of a macheté, retaining his crouch until he could come back up drawing almost a yard of steel from his cane. Twice that steel shot out like a viper's tongue. No sound escaped his opponent but he, too, went down, sprawled back on the roof as his companions moved in, trying to circle the Albino and take him from behind.

The faces of the remaining attackers were as dead as the first. The eyes barely moved but were fixed unblinkingly on their would-be victim. Zenith recognized them as readily as the others. All were petty crooks familiar to anyone who spent time in certain parts of the East End. And he knew for certain who had sent them against him. With a low laugh he let the distance between himself and the zombi shorten.

"So, Mississippi Jim, we meet for the last time. Do you remember vowing to kill me all those years ago on Lindisfarne?" He laughed softly. Most other men, however brave, would have known fear in this situation, but Zenith seemed actually to be enjoying himself. He laughed again as Mississippi Jim, the whites of his eyes swallowing his distended pupils, moved in for the kill.

The bitter wind was so fierce it almost drove Zenith off his feet and he paused for a moment, gathering balance and strength. Then his powerful muscles and extraordinary sense of balance, which had allowed him to stay at liberty in more than one seemingly impossible situation, came into play. This time the macheté was whirled like a bandmaster's baton by a huge creature with the same dead features as the others, an unnatural balance as it shuffled in for the kill. Zenith felt the rush of air as the cruel steel narrowly missed his face.

Ducking, the Albino put out the flat of his left hand and shoved. The zombi staggered backward, recovered its footing, lunged at Zenith, who stepped aside, putting out one patent leather shoe so that his opponent threw his arms forward, dropped the macheté and flew almost gracefully into the darkness as the train sped on. Zenith dropped to one knee, recovering himself and waiting for a fresh attack. It never came.

The Albino drew his cape around him against the cold, then straightened to his full height. He moved with all the grace of a Russian ballet master back towards the rattling gap through which he had recently ascended. Almost carelessly, he swung back down the train and dropped through the window, turning to fasten it. Then he opened the communicating door to the dining car and went in.

To the Albino's surprised, the two older ladies were still seated, apparently oblivious of what had gone on over their heads, but of Vespa there was no trace!

Zenith frowned. A question formed on his lips, but since the women did not look up, he shrugged and returned to Vespa's compartment. He knocked. There was no reply. He knocked again, softly calling her name. Silence.

With growing concern, Zenith turned the door handle. The door was not locked. He called her name softly before entering. Still no reply. Her compartment was made up for the night. A popular magazine lay on the bunk. Soft lamps burned overhead. Everything looked perfectly normal.

Except Vespa was not in her compartment.

Instead, on the bed, where he was bound to see it, lay a single sheet of creamy white paper. In a good but foreign hand a few words had been written on it.

M'sieu: If you continue to pursue your present course, your lady friend will meet the same fate as those you fought recently.

There was no signature.

A faint smile crossed the Albino's lips as he crumpled the paper in his hand.

Whoever had kidnapped Vespa had made an inexcusable mistake.

Up to now Zenith had joined in this adventure more for amusement than for profit. But no one attacked a man, woman or child, whom the Prince of Crime had chosen to protect. The game had become serious.

He chose not to jump from the train at that stage. His car was in a goods wagon and he had the feeling he would need it.

There was little to be gained from hasty action. He now had unfinished business in Paris.

He returned to his own compartment where Oyami prepared first three pipes of opium, then his bath and finally his bed. Whereupon the Albino fell into a brief deep sleep.

Later, as the express steamed into Paris-Nord station, Zenith put his head out of the window, signalling for a porter. He had decided on a course of action. All he had was a name, for Vespa had promised to give him the rest of the information on their arrival, but he would stay in Paris, as planned.

Oyami drove him from the station to the Place de la Republique. The morning traffic was busy and slow but thanks to Oyami's expertise with the wheel, they soon arrived at the Hotel Bristol, which Zenith favoured. It was a quiet hotel, known for the opulence of its appointments and the discretion of its staff. "She knew we were on her trail and chose to declare war on Zenith," he said to himself as soon as Oyami had tipped the porter. "I suppose she must be taught what it means to challenge me."

And with that he began to make his plans.

CHAPTER SIX
Yvette on the trail

MLLE YVETTE'S FIRST line of investigation was classic detective work. She went to see the surviving relatives. Two were in Mayfair, within easy walking distance. The other was in the country, south east of London.

Her first call was to Albemarle Court, a block of expensive flats in the style known as 'red brick Gothic', the town address of the Hon. Arthur Price, youngest son of the Viscount Broadmore. The relatively modest blocks of flats had been built as town apartments for people living most of the time in the country who did not wish the upkeep of a town house. They housed a rather disproportionate number of younger sons and unmarried daughters who did not wish to live on their parents' country estates and could not afford places of their own.

Mr Price's apartment was on the second floor. There was no lift, but the stairs did not present a problem to the athletic young woman. She had gathered that his sister had looked after the funeral arrangements, leaving a manservant in the apartment to work out his month's notice dealing with any eventualities arising while the place was vacant.

Yvette was at her most winsome in interviewing the servant who was won over by her charm. She was invited in and waited while he brought in tea and sat down across from her to pour it. She had already noticed the sporting prints and other signs of an interest in the track and the ring and as she sipped a rather good Darjeeling asked some pertinent questions. The man's name was Turpin and he had been in Price's employ for several years.

"So your gentleman was interested in sport, I see, Mr Turpin. Huntin'. Shootin' and fishin', as they say."

"Well he didn't do very much, miss. I think he rode to hounds as a young man, but I wouldn't say he was very athletic. His interest was more as a spectator, I'd say."

"Horses and such?"

"Yes, miss, that's right. All the big races. Epsom, Goodwood, Yarnton, Newberry." For some reason his normally ruddy features flushed redder and he made an involuntary movement of his hand, pushing the black hair back from his face.

She had noted a newspaper turned back to the sports pages. "You, too, are a follower of the sport of kings, I see."

"Oh, no, miss. Well, I did pick up a bit of an interest in racing from Mr Price, but I don't have the money to risk on a flutter. I've seen what that does to too many others."

He spoke feelingly and instinctively Yvette pressed this point. "You're not a gambling man, then, I take it."

"If I follow the horses, miss, it is to remind myself how rarely you win and how often you lose. Besides, I am still awaiting quite a bit in back wages."

"Mr Price was a poor payer?"

"Oh, he could be very generous on occasions, miss. But I'll admit he was a bit erratic when it came to the matter of my receiving my wages on time."

"Yet he received a regular stipend, I assume, from his family."

"Every month, miss."

"Then, I should have thought..." Yvette was already beginning to get a sense of Mr Price and his situation.

Turpin almost squirmed at this. "It wasn't really his fault, miss. I mean, he meant well. And he was a very generous, likeable man when in funds!"

"He gambled, I take it."

"Um, yes, miss. He did. Horses mostly."

"What else?"

"Anything he got a tip for – boxing, the Boat Race, the dogs – but every day it was the horses."

"He had a bookmaker?"

"Collins, miss. He calls himself Lucky Collins. And I suppose he is lucky – on his own account. Not so lucky for his customers."

"Did he have men – tough men – who worked for him?"

"I never saw them if he did. He really did try to pay his debts, miss. He cared about his family name and all that. Why, I'm not sure, since they never seemed to help him. He had to sell his blue china and his collection of prints quite recently. He was always apologising. But I thought he was getting out of the woods, so to speak. He once assured me that his will made sure I'd get every penny I was owed. He seemed to have a premonition. As if he knew he was ill and expected to die. Yet I've never seen him more cheerful in those last days."

"You don't suspect –?"

"Oh, it wasn't suicide, miss. He wasn't at all the type. Happy-go-lucky most of the time. Just an unfortunate coincidence."

"Did he have a poor relationship with his father?"

"Not really, miss. A matter of lifestyle, really. Lord Broadmore was a sporting gentleman himself. Wagered on all the big races. After Mr Arthur died his lordship settled all his debts. He could afford it. Mr Price felt strongly about paying his creditors. He did his best to pay what he owed. He tried to keep away from the track, but even when he went home it was almost impossible. His lordship said it was the company he kept. They all drank at a big pub in the area. He was always sure of making a 'big killing' and promising to double my wages. That sort of thing." Clearly Turpin had held his master in strong affection.

The manservant's eyes began to fill with tears so that Yvette reached out a gloved hand, placing it on his arm by way of comfort. "I'll not trouble you any further, Mr Turner, except to ask you for the address of Mr Price's parents."

"It's just his father now, miss. Viscount Broadmore, Hayling Castle, down in Surrey. I have a phone number somewhere."

While Turpin went to find the number Yvette looked swiftly around the room for anything which might help her, finding only a few curios on the mantelpiece: the usual things you picked up on a cruise but which seemed untypical of Price. A tiny skeleton of a monkey, a couple of phials of coloured sand, another phial, but empty, a plate with a picture of Havana, Cuba. "Your gentleman was a traveller, I see."

"Hardly, Miss. I do think he spent a bit of time in America, but he never spoke of it much. He was more your man about town, really."

Yvette thanked the manservant and left. She frowned as she made her way to the next address, the widow of Sir George Ogg, the JP. Like Price's family, she had not been informed yet of her husband's 'resurrection'. Also, as with Mr Turpin's master, there was no evidence that he had returned home. Lady Ogg was rather younger than Yvette had expected. She was not yet thirty, her raven-black hair was fashionably waved and her red afternoon dress was in the latest style. A pleasant, rather ordinary face. She wore only a little make-up and smiled pleasantly when Yvette entered the room into which she was had been shown.

"I apologise for keeping you waiting Miss –" she glanced at Yvette's card – "Bouvier. Are you from the insurance company?"

"I hope there will not be any delay, Lady Ogg." Yvette found it convenient to let the young woman believe what she had assumed. "There are just a few questions I need to ask you. Did your husband have any intimation of his coming death?"

Lady Ogg darted a startled look in Yvette's direction, "He seemed in perfect health. The only reason he took out the insurance was, he said, to give me security."

"You feared you would be unable to manage if Sir George died?"

Lady Ogg fiddled with her handkerchief. "Well, it probably wasn't much of a secret. We are – were – not especially wealthy people, Miss Bouvier. My husband, as a JP, had no income and we had invested rather badly in a copper company – the Fulbright Mine? You've no doubt heard of it?"

"Of course." As someone who had suffered from the crooked manipulation of stock, Yvette knew very well what had happened. There had been a massive crash when it was discovered that Fulbright stock was worthless. The mine had been 'dry' before the stock had been issued. Fulbright himself was now in gaol in Brazil. His partner had shot himself. Most of his victims were uncompensated. Only a few had invested all their money in a scheme which, to Yvette, felt too good to be true. She was genuinely sympathetic. "A terrible affair. So many innocent people affected."

"Quite. George learned of the scheme from someone at his club. Apart from some small flutters on the major flat races, he wasn't profligate but he was perhaps a little innocent. The Fulbright wasn't the first scheme he had bought into. We were living a little beyond our means, with our country house as well as this one, and he put pretty much all our liquid assets on, as he put it, the Fulbright's nose. You can imagine how he felt when we got the news. I believe that is what killed him." Again her handkerchief was lifted to her face. "But my husband was incapable of suicide. We would have sold this house, perhaps, and looked around for something more modest. But the strain was greater than I imagined... We had some land which we had hoped to lease for shooting, but it needed restocking and we simply could not afford..."

Yvette began to feel a little guilty at her unintended deception. She asked for the address in the country and shook hands before leaving. There was still time to get down to the Earl of Morn's house, so she decided to drive, taking the Dover Road and branching off well before she reached the sea, heading for the pretty market town of Callshott. The Earl of Morn's manor was reached by an unmade road and clearly little work had been done on the place for years. Outbuildings were in a state almost of ruin. The house itself had not seen a paintbrush or been repointed in years. It was so neglected, in fact, that Yvette thought it abandoned. As she got out of her car, Yvette thought she saw a face appear briefly at an upstairs window. Reaching the door, she feared the bell might come away in her hand as she pulled. A distant clanging was followed by a shuffling noise and eventually an ancient butler, wearing his green baize apron, opened the door. He did not look welcoming.

Yvette proffered her card and politely asked if she might have a word with the lady of the house. He ignored her hand and instead growled at her in a very aggressive way. "I've told you all before, her ladyship is too ill to deal with you. She was recently bereaved. You'll get your money, you bloodsuckers, when the insurance pays up!"

"Actually, I was hoping to speak to Lady Morn. I'm not a dun, I assure you."

"You're not from the bookmakers?"

"Indeed I am not. I am a private detective who wishes —"

"Send her away, Nutbrown! It's a trick. They'll try anything. I am sick and tired of the deceptions those leeches use to get their money. We'll pay when the insurance pays and not before. Now be off with you, gel, or I'll take a shotgun to you. I still have enough strength to load a gun!"

Yvette rather admired the lady's attitude and, having no time to find out if the threat was empty or not, got into her car and turned it in the overgrown driveway. She had discovered the rather significant fact that all three men had been in financial difficulties and bought insurance policies not long before they had apparently died. Now it looked as if they had been involved in a plan to defraud the insurance companies of at least enough to pay their outstanding gambling debts. With a sigh she drove out of the grounds and pulled in beside a grass verge to check the best way home. To her surprise she realized that all the men had lived relatively close together on the borders of Surrey and Kent. And almost equidistant from them all was the town of Yarnwell. And just outside Yarnwell stood the country house known as Yarn Abbey.

And Yarn Abbey, as Yvette well knew, was the house of Dr Huxton Ryman and Molly Dent, living as Professor Michael Butterworth and his niece!

"It might be nothing but coincidence but if so it will be the second. Two coincidences begin to seem more than accidental." Yvette pressed her dainty foot to the accelerator pedal and headed for the crossroads where a sign gave Yarnwell as 12 miles to the West. She wondered whether she should push on back to London or follow her hunch. Minnie, her receptionist, might be wondering where she was. It was just past 4pm so she drove on until she reached the next village. There she went into the post office and made a telephone call to say she was unlikely to be back until that evening. Satisfied that Minnie would not worry, she returned to her car and drove into the pretty old market town of Yarnwell just as it began to grow dark.

The Cross Keys, a pleasant coaching inn, rather larger than was probably needed these days, was already lighting its gas as she turned into the courtyard to be welcomed by the landlord himself, a little surprised to see that a young lady on her own was behind the wheel of the powerful two-seater. When she enquired about a room the big, swarthy man laughed heartily.

"Bless you, miss. You can have any room you like. We don't get a lot of business this time of the year no more and you're very welcome. We can cook you a decent high tea if that suits you – some local ham, a couple of eggs, a sausage or two and some fried potatoes. Simple fare but my wife's a passable cook and I guarantee it'll be tasty. It's only what we'll eat ourselves."

Yvette had developed a taste for simple English cooking of this type and she nodded enthusiastically. "I would imagine you don't get the customers you did when coaches still passed this way." From the boot she pulled the small suitcase she always kept packed for these occasions.

"Oh, we still get coaches during the season, only it's motor coaches now, of course. They come for the racing."

"Of course!" She felt a little silly not to have made the association. "Yarnton Park. Where they run the Duke of Coln's Cup, among others."

"That's right, miss. Gets crowded during the flat season and to tell you the truth I rather like it when it's quiet like this. Shall you be staying for the one night?"

On the spur of the moment, Yvette had decided to stay. "I think so. Is there somewhere I can put my car."

He was rather proud of the Inn's modern facilities directing her to a converted stable as he took her case inside.

There were still a couple of hours to go before 'high tea' so Yvette, inspecting the map, decided to take, she said, a stroll. She thought she might go and look at Yarn Abbey since she had never visited it. It was only half-an-hour's walk at most from the town. Telling the landlord that she would be back in time for her supper, she set of along the road, rather enjoying the smells of this 'season of mellow fruitfulness' as she strolled beneath tall, overhanging oaks and elms and soon found herself at the house's gates, which were locked shut.

Rather than alert Ryman and Molly of her presence, no matter how innocent, Yvette walked around the old sandstone wall until she found a   wicket gate over which she could climb. She found herself approaching the lovely old manor from the rear.   The landlord of the inn had told her that 'Professor Butterworth', and his niece were nice enough people, always giving a generous donation to carol-singers and such but otherwise keeping themselves to themselves.

It was growing dark as Yvette moved softly through the undergrowth, surprised that so few lights had come on in the house. Here, in the walled gardens at the back, was a cluster of large greenhouses bigger than those normally found in the grounds of such houses. Apparently recently constructed, they were sturdily made. She wondered idly if Ryman were cultivating roses for the Yarn Show, which the landlord had also mentioned.

Still unsuspicious, Yvette drew closer, a story ready in case anyone saw her. She had no idea why she was here, except she followed one of her famous hunches. She decided not to hide herself. That way anyone seeing her would believe her story about getting lost and needing directions.

She was prepared for a voice to call from the house, asking her why she was trespassing.

What she was not prepared for, as she drew closer, was the sound of gunshots fired in rapid succession.

They came from inside the house. Quickly, Yvette drew into the shadow of a wall, her heart suddenly beating rapidly. Another shot. Raised voices. And then the sound of running feet crunching on gravel. She did her best to get out of sight. Were they shooting at her ?

Suddenly, Yvette rather wished she had brought her pistol. As it was, she was completely unarmed and had no way of defending herself if whoever it was with the gun decided to take a shot at her!

CHAPTER SEVEN
Seaton Begg Smells a Rat

THE FOLLOWING MORNING, when Seaton Begg arrived at the office, he was surprised to discover their somewhat distraught assistant, Minnie Jones, waiting for him on the step.

"It's Mlle Yvette, Mr Begg. She told me she'd telephone from where she was staying. The line was rather crackly and I couldn't hear well. She was at a very nice hotel in the country. Someone called Abby was helping her. Apparently she told good yarns. She was going to follow up on a story, I think, by checking on an old house she was interested in. Honestly, Mr Begg, I did my best to listen. I made notes. She didn't seem worried about anything. She was in her car. I know she had planned to be back by yesterday evening but her telephone call said she would be back this morning."

"Well, surely there's no need to worry just yet, Miss Jones. Mlle Yvette has scarcely been gone for twenty hours," began Begg.

At that moment the door of his own offices opened suddenly from the inside and Winker Watson, very pale, stood there. "Chief. I think you'd better come in. You, too, Minnie."

Begg soon learned that Winker had been first in to the office that morning. He had found an envelope pushed under the front door. It read: This is not your affair. No harm will come to your woman if you will stay back. If you do not, then she will die.

Begg promptly went into his office, telling the others to follow him. When all were seated he said: "This could be part of the same case. One on which we're working, as you know Winker, in close association with Scotland Yard, the Quai des Orfèvres, and Washington. But it's unlike Yvette knowingly to take part of our case before we all agreed it between us!"

90

"Maybe she didn't know it, chief. Or didn't have time to tell us anything. What clients did she have here yesterday, Minnie?"

"Just the one. A Mr Jarvis. See, she had me write it down in the day book. She brought him in first thing yesterday morning. She'd met him in the street apparently. I think he's from around here. He looked as if he'd just stepped out. No hat and no overcoat…"

"So we must assume she took the case and began work immediately. A matter of urgency. Hmm. We'd better look for any notes she kept."

In Yvette's office the jottings she had made when interviewing Jarvis were still there. She had no doubt transferred the salient details to her notebook. Begg frowned over the neatly written foolscap sheet: Jarvis. Local fun. 3 missing. 2 local, 1 Surrey.

"Not much, really. Jarvis lives in this part of London. He's what? A comedian? Organises local 'fun'. What kind? Maybe for children –?"

But Winker was going through Yvette's Kelly's Directory. "Here it is, chief! Jarvis Sons and Jarvis – Funeral Directors."

"I wonder if he's missing three corpses, Winker?"

"Oo!" exclaimed Minnie, sitting down.

Begg smiled thinly. "You stay here and listen for the telephone, Miss Jones. In case Mlle Yvette calls again. We'll go to see this Mr Jarvis."

Once on their way to Albemarle Row Begg outlined what he had discovered about the two men from French Tony's. "It's a Voodoo cult, all right, Winker, though a much corrupted one. Those two men who were shot were part of it, recruited in Paris. They were in some way killed, then brought back to life. What actually happened, I'm pretty sure, is they were turned into a state resembling hibernation. A type of curaré was used."

"Gosh, chief, that's the stuff in South America that stops you breathing, doesn't it?"

"Some strains are more virulent than others. I suspect hypnotism was also used to control them in this case. They were hypnotized and ordered to do what, thank goodness, they failed to do — to kill someone at Tony's, probably Ryman or Zenith…"

"But how did they leave the police morgue, chief? Both men had bullets in the brain and one was also shot in the heart. They got into a boat, apparently!"

"That, I suspect, has a prosaic answer rather confused by the report of a drunkard. Chances are the witness was also hypnotised I can think of no other explanation. Coutts and I are working closely with the French and American police who also have evidence of Voodoo practices. Previously, we assumed the cult was made up of people of African origin. But all cases reported are of Europeans. The French also believe the head of the cult is a woman and from everything I have been told I have to conjecture that we know her, Winker!"

"Not Marie –?"

"Marie Leveaux the so-called Voodoo Queen. Precisely. Until now she has confined herself mostly to the Americas – Yucatan, Argentina, the Caribbean, as we know from our earlier cases, but I'm certain it is she and that she is either in Paris or London as we speak. And of course she believes Yvette is working directly with us. I think Marie kidnapped her to make us stop our investigation. A serious mistake. Now we must discover where she's hiding – and pray that Yvette is there. Let us hope Mr Jarvis can throw some light on this business!"

They had now reached Albemarle Row and had no difficulty discovering the discreetly advertised premises of Jarvis Sons and Jarvis. Apparently only one Mr Jarvis remained.

That gentleman's appearance was very little different from when Yvette had interviewed him. He was very glad to see Begg, assuming that the detective had also come in on the case. "There's only one Jarvis left, I fear, Mr Begg." He uttered a rusty laugh. "Too many Jarvis daughters. All married and flown the nest now. The staff are no longer related. Once you could have called out 'Mr Jarvis' and have a dozen heads turn in the embalming room alone."

At Begg's request he reiterated his story of the previous day, leaving the detective frowning. "So where did they go, I wonder."

"I wish them no ill, Mr Begg, but I would be glad to have them back and before next Thursday, if you could."

"That might not be possible, Mr Jarvis. I believe you are the victim of a particularly unpleasant deception. But if we solve this case I assure you, your reputation will remain unsullied."

"I'm grateful for that, Mr Begg."

As he had done on the previous day, Mr Jarvis again supplied the names and addresses of the three dead men. Begg and Winker were soon following in Yvette's footsteps. Now, however, there was greater urgency for they were also seeking a kidnapping victim.

The information the detectives gathered was the same Yvette had culled. Within the hour Begg, his assistant and Stone, the bloodhound were heading across the river in the Silver Spectre, her purring motor easily taking her to over sixty miles an hour as she ate the distance to Callshott Manor. There they were received much as Yvette had been received but Begg was persistent, giving the ancient butler his card and insisting he show it to his mistress.

In a few minutes the two detectives were led through the crumbling manor to a sitting room which smelled predominantly of cats, mould and lavender water. Seated on a decaying sofa, Lady Morn waited to receive them. Lord Morn had been a relatively young man, so they were surprised at his wife's somewhat advanced age. She was at least seventy and wore what had once been fashionable and expensive clothes. Now they were little more than stained rags.

The straight-backed old lady chuckled when she read the surprise in her visitors' eyes.

"Oh, yes, you expected to find a pretty little empty-headed thing, no doubt. Only, you see, Gordon didn't marry me for anything but my money. I knew that, though I didn't expect him to spend it so rapidly. He has a disease, I soon discovered, which no book warns you about and few doctors imagine. He is a gambler, gentlemen. He has thrown every penny away on cards, horses, dogs and boxing. When he died nothing was left of the estate. Everything's mortgaged to the hilt. When we have his funeral, the only mourners apart from myself will be his unpaid creditors."

"No doubt such a scoundrel would not provide you with life insurance," murmured Begg a little slyly.

"The odd thing is he did take out insurance on his life. I heard about it this morning. Quite a considerable sum. No doubt he expected me to remain here and put this damned house into shape. Well, I shall not. I am leaving as soon as possible to end my years with my cousin in the Bahamas. I warned that weak and cowardly man that I would!"

Begg could not help admiring the old woman's spirit. "You have no idea, I suppose, who his cronies were in these parts?"

"Any time he had he spent over at Yarnton Park where the racetrack is. All his friends were fair-weather — and all of them knew every public house in the Home Counties."

Begg's face suddenly brightened. Winker, who knew when his chief had an inspiration, said under his breath. "What's up, chief?"

Seaton Begg took a map from his pocket. He studied it briefly and then replaced it. "Well, thank you so much, Lady Morn. You have been of great assistance to us."

"Had that scoundrel done something actually against the law?" she wished to know, perhaps wanting her instincts to be confirmed.

"I rather think so, Lady Morn. But I'm not altogether sure you will be glad to know what it was. We'll see. Thank you for hospitality and your information. It has been very useful." Bowing, Begg turned and almost ran from the house.

As he put the car into gear, the detective whistled under his breath, a sure sign that his extraordinary intelligence was actively engaged on a solution to a problem. "It's all coming together, Winker, old son! There's a chance we can save the day yet. But we've fast work to do! We're up against a fiend of the first order!"

And with that he roared down the unkempt drive and swung out into the road, heading for Yarnwell.

CHAPTER EIGHT
Some Mysteries of Paris

ZENITH, HAVING HAD Oyami drape his rooms with black silk, lay upon an ottoman smoking his third pipe. The opium acted to help him dream of other things, distracting him from what he would

94

rather not dream about, but it also had the unusual effect of stimulating certain intellectual centres of his brain. While part of him escaped from his past, another part engaged with the moment.

He could guess exactly who had captured Vespa della Vulpa and why were they making war on him? No other person except Seaton Begg, had the kind of courage to risk making an enemy of him. He did not consider the police to be enemies. They were mere nuisances. This new enemy might not fear him simply because they did not know him well. This gave him a better sense of his opponent. A person who used kidnapping routinely as a persuasive tool.

No French or English criminal had that habit. This was more likely something you heard of in Sicily or perhaps Turkey − or America, of course. America? Zenith ran his keen mind over a catalogue of villains and villainy, but no other name came to him. A formidable opponent.

In his mind he reviewed what little information Vespa had given him to whet his appetite for the adventure. Something rare and exotic which could make countless millions for those who owned it? Something to be found in Paris. A Spaniard called Blasco. What had she said as they danced? Something about the Chateau de Verre. The Glass Castle! He thought she had been speaking rhetorically. But now −

Was there some Parisian equivalent of, say, the Crystal Palace in London? No, the Eiffel Tower, built for another great exhibition, was scarcely the same. The Maison de Verre had been announced as a coming Parisian architectural project but was yet to be built. Was there some scandal attached to this which Vespa planned to exploit?

At length Monsieur Zenith rose, refreshed, from his couch. "This afternoon, Oyami," he murmured, addressing his white-clad servant. "I shall stroll the boulevards and think."

Careless that his likeness adorned the bulletin boards of every gendarmerie in Paris, the Albino strolled insouciantly forth.

95

Growing bored with the familiar faces and places of his old stamping grounds, M. Zenith took coffee at a little table in the Luxembourg Gardens and read *Le Monde*. Coming across a story concerning the beautiful mosque recently built as thanks for the thousands of Moslem soldiers who had helped France in the Great War, Zenith had a whim to see the place again. "Then I shall take some refreshing mint tea in the little café attached to the *Grande Mosquée de Paris*."

Oyami set him down a few yards from the mosque across the road from the *Jardin des Plantes*. Entering the calm beauty of the mosque, Zenith scarcely glanced at the entrance to the   botanical gardens. An old *mula* came forward to show him the   glories of the building with its decorative tiles and calligraphy. He paused for a while to enjoy the tranquility of the blue and grey water garden and eventually strolled to the *salon de thé* with its gorgeous tiles arranged in patterns to represent plants and flowers. Here he ordered tea, poured for him by skillful waiters in the now traditional tarboosh and whites of their calling. Zenith recalled how he loved to relax in the shadowy calm. The tiles reflected light from a dozen indirect sources., listening to the music of the water from a variety of fountains. He only occasionally felt so tranquil. It seemed to Zenith that something fundamental was expressed by the sparkling fountains which added to the building's peace and his own appreciation of water, without which little in the world would exist.

After taking tea, Zenith felt unusually at ease. He remained focused on finding and rescuing Vespa, but decided to take a walk in the botanical gardens to think things through before going back to his hotel. The Jardin des Plantes contained flowers and shrubs from all over the world. In their autumn colours, their scents combined subtly in wonderful harmony. Zenith stared rather critically at the classical stone of the museum and the Victorian tropical greenhouse beside it: two styles which did not go naturally together. Then, as he turned away he suddenly cursed himself for an oaf.

Of course! She had spoken, perhaps, not of an actual glass castle but of something called that in the popular vernacular! Almost certainly it was this one, since there was little like it in Paris proper. Now he smiled to himself. But what could be so valuable here that it would make them millionaires?

He thought of the tulip thefts and trade in bulbs that had once gone on in Holland. Maybe that great hothouse contained some rare plant more valuable than diamonds? The 'Castle of Glass' lay before him, tantalizing his imagination, exuding tropical scents so delicious and sensual that one could almost swim in them, float on them. Through the glittering glass Zenith saw the brilliantly coloured flowers, the lush greens, subtle and varied, the sense of exotic animals and people who once roamed thousands of miles of such jungles.

Almost in a trance, Zenith pushed open the door and walked through. For a moment the heat almost took his breath away. He raised his hat to an astonished young woman on his left. It was not often that the great tropical greenhouse was visited by a man in full evening dress!

Barely aware of the sensation he caused, Zenith stepped along the central boardwalk until he reached a door which had stencilled on it in French:

> *Dr Jesus BLASCO. No admittance. Experimental work in progress.*

The name Vespa had whispered! he knew. But why had she wanted them to meet?

Without hesitation, Zenith turned the knob and stepped through into a large, well-lit laboratory, as hot as the plant house outside. Frowning, he glanced swiftly around him. The laboratory was empty. He had hoped that Blasco could help him find Vespa. Evidently there had been a struggle, judging by the disturbed and overturned terracotta planters and green seed boxes once arranged in rows everywhere. It was also easy to see that some sort of search had taken place. Dark earth was scattered across benches and floors. Plants had been ripped from their pots and abandoned.

There were also a few drops of blood. Zenith knew he looked at signs of a struggle. Two or three men had attacked the scientist as he worked. What were they looking for? Something hidden in the pots? Precious stones, perhaps? Glass? A slang word for diamonds...

Swiftly, Zenith checked what he found on the floor. No clue to the contents of the pots. Then his eyes fell on something – a single petal. He picked it up, recognizing it. He smiled as only he could smile.

"*Le Narcisse Noir,*" he murmured. "The Black Narcissus. I saw one long ago in Port au Prince. Aha! Now I begin fully to understand." He frowned thoughtfully. "I need to pay a visit to Hispaniola Luc. Let's hope he still lives in Belleville." Zenith picked up the delicate petal and put it carefully in his waistcoat pocket. As he turned to leave, the door suddenly burst open and the young woman he had seen earlier appeared, pointing him out to a middele-aged gendarme who stood there, a look of astonishment on his face.

"*Zenith!*"

The Albino was almost as well-known to the French police as he was to the British.

Sardonically, Zenith again lifted his hat to the young woman and offered the policeman a thin smile. "*Enchanté, ma'mselle – m'sieu.*"

The policeman lifted his whistle to his lips but all his breath was gone for the moment. At once, the Albino's sword cane left its ebony sheath. The poor gendarme stepped back, eyes wide, with some view of protecting the lady. His movement was unnecessary for Zenith had darted past him and on light feet reached the exit and was through the outer door before the pair could follow. By the time they reached the outside they saw the lithe figure of the Albino running along the path to the gates where Oyami waited in his car.

98

Another moment and an exhilarated Zenith had fallen back laughing into the seat of his limousine. "Belleville, Oyami," he said. "Rue Haxo. Quickly, please!"

An hour later, an unshaven, bleary-eyed man of Creole descent stumbled into the cheap room he rented on the top floor of Madame Boulet's boarding house. As was usual for him at this hour he was somewhat the worse for drink or drugs, having some difficulty in opening the door. As he turned on the gas he saw in annoyance that his skylight was open to the early evening air. His hand reached for the string which would close the window but before he could complete the movement he felt a firm, cool hand on his shoulder and looking around realized that he was not alone. He gasped. "*Mais non*! *Le Phantom Blanc!*" Terrified, he spoke with a strong Haytian accent. His knees threatened to buckle. When he felt the point of a sword at his throat he could barely stand. "M'sieu. I beg you. Spare me! When have I ever betrayed you?"

"Never, as far as I know, Hispaniola Luc. And I am sure that on this occasion you would wish to maintain that record. Is that not so, M'sieu Luc?"

"Always, m'sieu."

"Bon. I need you to tell me where the Sorceress holds her séance tonight!"

"Oh, *M'sieu le Phantom* My life, it would be the end for him if I told you."

"Come, come, Luc, you know your life is already worthless. It is only because I choose it that you live! Now, you filth. Tell me what I wish to know."

In spite of his normal skin tones Hispaniola Luc grew almost as pale as the Albino. He tried hard to keep his secret but it was not long before Zenith had the information he needed and was gone by the same route as he had entered.

The full moon had risen high in the sky when, at a certain old house in Montmartre, its high-walled back garden hidden from sight of any neighbor, a tall pale man in evening dress and wearing smoked glasses joined a group of similarly-clad men and their women. This was a group drawn from among the noblest families in France. They were here to witness a forbidden and terrifying ritual utterly at odds with all Christian principles and beliefs: a form of devil-worship particularly foul precisely because it was enjoyed by men and women thought to be among the most highly civilized in the world. They now formed a circle beneath the awning of a heavy pavilion which further concealed their activities from any eyes but their own. The canvas sides, painted with symbols Coutts would have recognized as the same as those he found in Hyde Park, also muffled any sound coming from within the great tent.

From a doorway in the house more dark figures, their half-naked bodies painted in certain colours, brandished long jungle knives polished to mirrors and of vicious sharpness. They flashed in the light of flickering brands held by the guests. Then the dancers drew back to reveal a terrified girl of hardly sixteen summers, in a ragged school frock, all that remained of her uniform, tied to a triangular frame with her hands bound above her head. Her dark red hair was damp with sweat. Her brown eyes were hot with fear and she had something wrong with her throat, for when she tried to scream no sound emerged.

Without doubt she had been given a weak solution of *curaré*, freezing her vocal chords.

The tall man in smoked glasses allowed his flute to be filled with champagne but refused the other drugs being passed around by liveried Africans with blank eyes and fixed grins. No one questioned his presence there because no guest ever questioned another at the *La Maison aux Sorciéres*.

From the periphery came the sound of soft, sinister drumming and then, appearing as if from nowhere, a massive negro in European white tie and tails, a tall silk hat on his head, began to dance gracefully before the writhing child. A whisper went round the circle: *"Baron Samedi! Baron Samedi!"*

Wielding a glinting cutlass, the man called 'Baron Samedi' dropped to his knees in front of the tied-up girl. Then another figure materialized: A woman, masked like an angel, her gorgeous, body clad in rippling black silk, black feathers and scarlet blossoms.

Now the drumming grew faster, more frenzied, and 'Baron Samedi' began to pass his cutlass back and forth before the girl's neck, murmuring words which everyone there recognized yet would seem gibberish to any stranger.

The woman lifted her head in a chant which thrilled the blood of almost all who listened.

Her brown body gyrated suggestively before her audience. She, too, brandished a long knife. From somewhere another dancer stepped forward holding a black-plumed cockerel, its struggling mirroring that of the captive girl. The movements of the dancers further excited the audience of jaded socialites who murmured their appreciation.

Then the blade slashed at the bird and suddenly blood was gouting from the severed neck. The dancers gasped their pleasure. Some of them were stripping all their outer garments and joining in the sensual humming and swaying, rocking back and forth on their heels, gasping their appreciation as 'Samedi' next nicked the girl's soft throat with the tip of his cutlass. The Sorceress laughed and tasted the blood on the blade, showing her appreciation as the audience bayed its disgusting desires.

Another silent scream from the girl and their response was laughter – weird, crazed, excited! The laughter of the damned!

It was clear now that the child was to be cut to death slowly to entertain an audience greedy for her blood and her pain. A nick to her arm. Blood spurted as she frantically sought to escape. More laughter.

Then the white-faced man in smoked glasses did what he had not planned to do. With a sigh, as if he disapproved of his own sentimentality, he drew the slender blade from its ebony sheath. Then he sprang to the girl's side, stabbed 'Baron Samedi' in the throat, snatched the big African's cutlass from him and cut the girl's bonds, gathering her up in one lithe movement even before the audience realized this was not part of the fiendish 'entertainment'. He pushed the gyrating 'Sorceress' contemptuously aside, and disappeared out of the tent.

The guests milled about in confusion, not knowing precisely what was happening. And then, suddenly, they found themselves engulfed as heavy canvas descended on their heads. They were trapped and their movements became more agitated. Then the flames caught the canvas. Then they started to scream.

With a quiet chuckle of satisfaction, Zenith went back into the house, carrying the astonished girl in his arms. A few paces took him to the street door. He sped out into the narrow rue Machinot, hearing the increasingly urgent screams of the pseudo-Voodoo worshippers, and reached the busy Place Pigalle where a car with darkened windows awaited him.

Zenith had not gone to rue Machinot planning to rescue anyone. He had hoped to find Vespa della Vulpa or at least get information he could use in finding her. But he had found neither Vespa nor the woman he knew as 'the Sorceress'. The creature at the ceremony had not been she. He had learned enough, however, to know that the real Sorceress was probably not in Paris.

"Which means she has already left Paris," he mused. "If she ever left England!" The girl beside him shrank back from him, not knowing what he meant. He apologized and spoke in French. "Forgive me, my child." His tone was gentle, almost kindly. "Let me know where you will be safe and you shall be taken there."

Her throat still frozen, she croaked the name of a Carmelite convent near the Gare du Nord and Zenith nodded. "Did you hear that, Oyami?"

The Japanese inclined his head and swung the big car into a side street, heading towards the centre of the city. Zenith drew off his scarlet-lined cloak and placed it around the girl's shoulders. From his wallet he took a number of notes and put them in her hand. "You must be careful where you go alone in Paris in future." He returned his attention to his driver.

"And then, Oyami, we return to London. I suspect the true Sorceress is already there and we must hope Signorina Vespa is still alive! I have a plan which no doubt will appeal to our Haytian friend!"

CHAPTER NINE
Secrets of Yarn Abbey

SEATON BEGG'S MOUTH had hardened into a thin, determined line. As he pushed the Silver Spectre to maximum speed, leaving a trail of agitated dust behind him, he and Winker discussed what they had so far deduced.

"All those men attended the Yarnton Races and almost certainly were acquainted. I don't think it's a coincidence, Winker, that Hoxton Ryman's house is nearby? They would probably know him as Professor Butterworth, of course. There had to be a big prize for him to risk his parole. Whether he put an idea to them as a criminal plan or not is still to be decided." Begg's eyes concentrated on the road ahead. He was anxious to get to Yarn Abbey as soon as possible. Almost certainly Yvette's life depended on it.

"They faked their own deaths, didn't they, chief? Ryman probably invented a drug which made the recipient seem dead, even to an experienced doctor. That was why they could disappear from the country and later somehow collect the insurance money. Yet their spouses don't seem to be involved."

"My guess is that they all met at the Yarnton Races. We know that Ryman enjoys a bit of a flutter now and again. But I still don't understand his motive..."

"Could he have been in debt himself, chief? Maybe he cooked up this scheme to sell to the others? But why did they wake up too soon, all of them? Where did they go? And what has this to do with those other chaps – the crooks who were shot in French Tony's? Did they also wake up too soon, figure they'd been double-crossed and decide to kill him? Seems a bit extreme, doesn't it?"

"If that's what happened, Winker. I'm sure they all met at or near the race track. Maybe in Yarnwell? I'm not sure if they knew Peter Hess the forger or Alphonse LeGris, the plastic surgeon. Presumably they would have wanted their services. Ryman could have known them from his criminal days. Someone was needed, of course, to supply fresh papers and identities. Fresh faces. Hess and LeGris were the right men for *that* job."

"Not a coincidence, surely? Yet I can't see Ryman being so broke that he'd get involved."

"I agree. But I do suspect Yvette's case and ours are indeed separate on one level. For the moment we had best concentrate on Yarn Abbey and what's going on there. In my mind there's no doubt that one important link is our old antagonist, Marie Levaux, the so-called 'Voodoo Queen'. We know she has three main gangs – one in the Americas, one in England and the other in France. We know the 'Voodoo' they practice is a complete corruption of the real ceremonies. Probably her intention is to draw in members of high society. They can then be blackmailed to help in her crimes, to fund them or to cover them up."

"But how, chief?"

"She is doubtless using drugs or hypnotism – probably both, as always. But why is Ryman risking getting mixed up with her again? I'm not sure. The last I knew, she was furious with Ryman for consorting with other women. She was ready to kill him when he made it clear that he and Molly were not going to separate. Marie swore to have nothing more to do with him."

"Do we know what area his research was in, chief?"

"The New York, London and Paris police are still trying to find out. Probably she renewed her acquaintance because she needed something from him. I have a fair idea what that is. His extraordinary abilities as a scientist once led him to study the effects of different kinds of *curaré*. No evidence yet, of course, that he was involved. And where Marie Levaux has been in recent days no one knows, either. Or rather there have been *too many* sitings of that beautiful fiend!" Begg took a bend in the road with almost reckless speed. "Some say they've seen her in Paris. Some believe that she's conducting her whole plan from London. She was even sighted in south east London, near Penge! Others have reported her as being in New York and New Orleans. She routinely employs doubles to give the impression of being in many places at the same time. One thing is likely – there are at least three females apparently heading a branch of the Voodoo cult in Britain, France and America. She lets people think that she is the only one. Thus she lends another apparently supernatural element to her mystique. Mlle LeVeaux manipulates her myth with considerable cunning. But where is she based? I suspect she recently moved her English headquarters and that they were in South London. Scotland Yard got too close. Coutts says they almost nailed her in Norwood."

"So why is she doing all this, chief? What's her game with the voodoo and so on?"

"I think she is experimenting with all forty or fifty kinds of *curaré*, a drug which suspends the nervous system and kills essentially by paralyzing the vital organs, most obviously the lungs. Effectively the victim 'drowns'. All her recent victims seemed dead – but weren't. That says *curaré* to me. Certain strains of the drug mimic natural causes. So I'm pretty sure I know the general circumstances behind those various 'deaths'. But what we don't know, Winker, is how they were restored to life! That's a much harder question to answer!"

"So the three men who walked out of that funeral parlour are just three pieces in a much larger puzzle?"

"Exactly! Messrs. Ogg, Morn and Price are, I suspect, hiding where Marie LeVaux is hiding now. Or somewhere nearby. I suspect if we find the 'Voodoo Queen' we'll find the three 'dead' men."

"Marie LeVeaux could be using Yarn Abbey as her base. Is that it, chief?"

"Not originally. I believe she probably was somewhere in the south eastern suburbs. She might have moved by now. But I'm not sure Ryman and Molly are willing hosts. They could be dead already. We know LeVeaux sent her *zombis* to French Tony's with orders to kill. She is no doubt also in a position to blackmail them. 'Professor Butterworth' and his 'niece' have much to lose if the police decide they've broken the terms of their parole."

"You're right there, chief," agreed Winker, as he thought it over. "And she's testing different kinds of *curaré* on different subjects. Is that what happened to Villeneuve and LeGris? Did she run out of subjects? After all, she needed them to complete her end of the bargain."

"Presumably they crossed her in some way. We both know from experience that Mlle LeVeaux is a passionate creature who frequently makes sudden, quixotic emotional decisions – loving fiercely at one moment – hating at another – often the same object. She was like that with Ryman, as we also know. I'm surprised she took up with him again. She must need his skills badly. If Hess the forger and Le Gris the surgeon refused her or challenged her in some way she could well have turned her *zombi* servants on them – then turned *them* into *zombis* herself!"

"Makes sense, chief! Aha! Here we are. Yarnwell three miles and Yarn Abbey four. Any minute now!"

But Begg was cautious, as Yvette had been the day before. When they arrived he parked the car in a little-used lane beneath some low-hanging willows so that it could not easily be seen from the road. "We'll leg it from here, Winker. Never approach from the front what can be approached from the side or back. But this time I want you to take Stone and let him nose around for Yvette. Meanwhile, I'll approach from the front and see what my instincts tell me. You know the drill."

"Right you are, chief. Come on, Stone boy." Calling the bloodhound, Winker set off, keeping a wall on his left. "Let's see where we can get in."

As soon as Winker had gone into the woods with Stone the bloodhound, Begg loosened his tie, unbuttoned his jacket and did his best to look like a casual caller out for a walk, or a man whose car had broken down. He wanted as many cover stories as possible.

Yarn Abbey was a weathered, well-kept manor of Norman origin, having been moated originally. The building had been substantially expanded in Tudor times. Its warm, decorative brick and half-timbering were especially pleasant. In the latter part of the 19th century, a Morris-influenced architect had restored and built on several attractive extensions. A harmony of warm stone, red brick, black timbers and dark green foliage, Yarn Abbey was one of the loveliest and oldest buildings in Kent, a county rich in great houses and castles, once the home of the Cinque Ports and consequently very rich until the tides drew out and did not come back as the harbours filled with silt.

Now Yarn Abbey had only memories of prosperous, noble families, save for Molly Dent's and a few others. Here 'Professor Butterworth' had his extraordinary laboratory where his work on cancer had already born tremendous advances fully justifying the Home Secretary's parole. As it happened, and quite ironically, Doctor Hoxton Ryman had ultimately done the human race far more good than harm!

Tramping up the well-kept drive Begg saw a big lorry parked to one side and noted the number. The side bore the name of a well-known private menagerie associated with supplying biological institutions with large animal specimens. There was a car parked next to it. It was not Yvette's. Were Ryman and Molly planning a get-away with all his equipment?

Then Begg walked up to the great double post-Gothic doors and pulled the bell.

He waited rather longer than he had expected before the door was opened by Ryman's butler, a large, red-faced man Begg recognized.

"Good afternoon, Baines. I'm not here to barge in on business at lunch-time. However, I'd rather hoped for a quiet word with your master. Any chance?"

Baines' eyes were a little glazed, as if waked from sleep. "Please wait here, sir, and I will discover if Professor Butterworth will see you. He's very busy with his radium experiments just now as you very likely know, sir. It's delicate and dangerous work and often cannot be interrupted. You appreciate that, sir."

"I do indeed, Baines. But fine work for mankind, I think, eh?"

"Quite, sir." The butler cleared his throat.

Begg was certain of it now: Baines was afraid and had been told to get rid of him without causing suspicion. Acting on impulse, the detective pushed past the butler, almost forcing his way into the hall, and there was Ryman himself, halfway down the great sweeping staircase and looking uncertainly at his visitor.

"Oh, hallo, Dr Begg. It's you, eh? Look here, I've got some work on and I'm pretty busy. If this is a social call I'm afraid I'm rather tied up. And poor Molly's also under the weather. She can't entertain you – "

"Tied up, too, is she?"

"Quite."

"I gather there's no chance of you putting me up until my car's fixed?"

"Exactly! I must apologise. So much on, you know."

This told Begg that Molly probably was actually tied up or otherwise restrained, not able to speak. By calling Begg 'Doctor", Ryman had alerted the detective to the fact that something was going on which he couldn't speak about. Probably somewhere in that house a gun was being held to her head. Everything that rogue genius had said indicated he was speaking under threat.

Begg's mind raced. He looked his old opponent straight in the eye. "Well, I suppose I'd best walk into Yarnwell and get a room there. Can you recommend anywhere?"

"People find the Cross Keys very comfortable." Ryman rubbed his eyes and made a brief sign. "There should be plenty of rooms now the racing season's over."

Begg had rarely seen him so desperate. "Thanks. I might drop in again before I go, if that's all right."

"Oh, of course, but you might not find us in. We're very busy, as I said."

"I'll take my chances. Well, goodbye, old boy. I'll be off, then. Oh, by the way, a mutual friend of ours was going to be motoring in these parts. Mlle Yvette Bouvier. You haven't seen her, have you?"

"Let me think. I remember the name." Ryman pretended to give the question consideration. "No. She probably went south. Very pretty this time of year."

"Thanks."

And with that, Begg had no choice but to let Baines open the door for him. A moment later he was walking back up the drive, hoping he had distracted whoever was watching, given Winker a chance to look around and Stone the opportunity to use his powerful nose.

The problem now was how to get back into Yarn Abbey without the occupants finding out.

As he walked slowly back up the drive, Begg felt he was being watched from both sides. He was thinking over what Ryman had said to him. Perhaps the most significant thing was his reference to Yvette whom, of course, he knew well. What had he meant when he said that she had 'gone down south'?

Then Begg had a brainwave. Of course! The basement in the south wing of the house! Yvette was almost certainly a prisoner there.

With this in mind, Begg did not walk back towards Yarnwell but instead turned to go further for a few hundred yards until he was certain as he could be that he was no longer being observed, then he got a foothold on the wall and levered himself up until he was able to drop down on the other side.

At this time of year the woods had the delicious smell of autumn, fecund and rich, full of rotting leaves and damp undergrowth. Begg trod carefully through this, making his way in a wide semi-circle until he had a good view of the house's south wing, built in Elizabethan times. There, in the cellars, Ryman had situated his laboratory. Begg was about to creep in further when suddenly he heard a commotion, some loud barking and a shouted order. Then came two shots – *bang, bang* – and the sound of someone running.

Before Begg had time to determine what was happening, Winker came haring into view, firing behind him at pursuing nightmare creatures who moved in a crouch, more like apes than men. All were barefoot. Some were white, others had negroid or Mongolian features, and all seemed to have been seamen by their clothing and general appearance.

Winker's shots were not wasted. While those he hit staggered and reeled a little, they continued to follow him, their lips frozen in fixed grins, their eyes glassy.

Relieved, Winker greeted Begg. "Am I glad to see you, chief! I don't know what those devils are, but they seem almost impervious to pistol shots."

"*Zombis*, Winker," his chief told him. "No doubt created by Marie LeVeaux through drugs and hypnotism from the poor devils who haunt every port and are never missed when they disappear. Gad! There's a swarm of them! A score at least." Begg's gun was in his hand now but he knew enough not to use it at that distance. The creatures could only be stopped at almost point blank range.

"Keep running, Winker!" Begg called urgently. "There are too many to fight."

Neither detective had realized that another pack of living dead men was approaching from behind. Begg risked a couple of shots but the creatures came on, lumbering like sleep-walkers, their long jungle knives raised menacingly.

But, for the moment at least, Begg and Winker were not to be chopped to pieces. The cold, dead-alive bodies crushed in on them so they could not have lifted their guns if they wished. This mass of cold, clammy flesh forced them back towards the house. Begg shuddered at their touch and felt physically sick. He had experienced these *zombi-men* more than once in the Caribbean. He had never expected to see them in Britain, nor in such numbers!

As they were pushed towards Yarn Abbey a woman emerged from the back door. She stood there, hands on her hips, grinning her triumph. With her dark skin and full red lips she was gorgeously beautiful, wearing a great white flower in her black, curly hair. Her frock, split to the thigh, was scarlet silk, flowing over her full figure. Her legs were shapely and she wore high-heeled shoes matching her dress. Although she employed doubles to add to her mystique, there was only one Marie LeVaux.

Willing to murder and torture to gain her ends, there was only one woman who had everything she had, including an utterly ruthless will to power which used her own people to further her selfish ends. Disbelieving any truth revealed about her, they followed her commands with fanatical loyalty and would have died for her.

"I'm sorry I involved you in this, old son," gritted Begg. For once he had led them into a situation from which there was little chance of escape. They had informed no one about their movements, so Coutts could not follow. They were in the power of creatures who could not be threatened with death. They were the captives of a woman who positively enjoyed torturing her terrified victims to death.

"I'm sorry, too, chief. I seem to have dropped the ball." Winker grunted as a hand on which the flesh flaked like leprosy pushed him in to the house while the woman chuckled her pleasure, going up close to Begg and touching his face, running her hands over his body as he did all he could to remain impassive and not show her the disgust he felt.

They were forced down some stairs into a space which had probably once been a series of cellars and was now fitted as a big laboratory.

There, in cages formerly used to house large experimental animals, stood Yvette, Molly Dent and Vespa della Vulpa, their hands tied above their heads, their feet barely touching the floor. Their faces were transformed by terror they could not disguise.

Down the stairs which led from the main house, came Dr Hoxton Ryman and Baines the butler, staggering as they were pushed in front of another dozen *zombi*-men. Marie LeVeaux's unstable laughter peeled through the echoing vaults. Her hand was on the shoulder of a bruised, shivering, unshaven little man with disheveled hair. It could only be Blasco the Spanish biologist, wearing a white coat stained with his own blood. He flinched away from her as she spoke. "Ah, it is good! The rest of my laboratory rats have arrived. We can soon begin our final experiments, eh, *mon amour?*"

She turned, her face full of passion. From the deep shadows, a mysterious smile on his handsome features, stepped a tall young man wearing his familiar evening dress.

"By heavens!" jerked Begg. "Of all men, I would never have believed you would have stooped to making such a filthy alliance!"

His crimson eyes gleaming like gemstones, Zenith the Albino shrugged and drew deeply on one of his opium cigarettes. "Needs must, you know Begg. Needs must…"

CHAPTER TEN
A Cure for Mortality

"MLLE LeVAUX HAS kindly agreed to a little bargain," said Zenith equably as he studied the scene before him. "We have become partners, so to speak, in crime. The drug known as CL14, synthesized from the black narcissus, will be patented by us and sold by a company we shall set up. I'm sure that you will applaud this decision in the spirit of free enterprise. But we have a problem with dosages and so on and that is why we have recruited Dr Jesus Blasco to our team," he indicated the frightened little man beside Marie LeVeaux. "And first, we have another clause in our contract to execute. My dear – "

"Vespa is of no further use to me. Once she told me where Blasco was all I needed her for was as 'bait' to bring my handsome Zenith, King of the Night, to me!" With studied carelessness, Marie LeVeaux plucked a jungle knife from the hands of one of her *zombis* and advanced to the cage where the three women were held. "Zenith found me at the Crystal Palace in South London. I had used a guard to allow me use a small portion of the great chamber to grow my plants." She tapped the Spanish scientist on his head. "I see you are surprised, Dr Blasco! You have been able to grow the black narcissi but in spite of all your attempts, using soil from the exact part of Hayti where it originally grew, you could never produce a sap which did what it should have done. You did not realize that *air* was as important as *earth*. Only the Crystal Palace is high enough to produce such air!"

One swift, accurate stroke of the knife – and the rope from which Vespa della Vulpa hung was severed. With a faint moan, the Italian dancer fell to the floor. Marie LeVaux laughed and spurned the adventuress with her foot. "You are free to leave. But remember, you will *always* be my creature, wherever you try to hide. Never be so foolish as to test yourself against the Voodoo Queen – and now her consort, Lord Zenith, the Voodoo King!" Laughing, she watched as the wretched Vespa dragged herself past the assembled *zombis* and up the steps, to vanish into the house.

"Voodoo King?" gritted Begg. "I can't believe that you, of all people, Zenith, have allowed yourself to get mixed up in this sordid, superstitious business!"

Zenith smiled again. "The operative word is 'business', my dear Begg, as indeed it has always been with my partner."

"And what partners we are," breathed the Creole woman. "We are truly the High Priest and Priestess of the Night, born to rule the dead and the undead. I have never known a man so thoroughly destined to be with me. How our followers will admire our beauty, our contrasts. Light and shadow. Good and evil. Law and Chaos – Life and Death! We have become all those things we represent. The basic balance of existence!" She began to busy herself with a tray of instruments, some stoppered phials and other pieces of medical equipment, assisted by Dr Blasco, the trembling, weeping biologist.

"That woman is mad," muttered Ryman. "I always suspected it."

"You'll hear no contradiction from me, Ryman." It was clear to Begg that Marie LeVeaux had, typically, transferred her passions again and become utterly fixated on the Albino as, quixotically, she had earlier 'loved' both Begg and Ryman.

Ryman was pale as he glared from behind the bars of the cage into which he, Begg, Baines and Winker, had been thrown. "If you let one woman go, why not free the others as well? Miss Dent has never done you harm. Neither has Mlle. Yvette! Why would you still be jealous of them? Monsieur Zenith is your true love now, as you have told us here repeatedly!"

"Oh, that is where you are wrong, Dr Ryman!" the Creole snarled. "I mean to start what I have finished. Those women insulted me, defied me – and stole from me."

"I don't understand," gritted Ryman. But she ignored him.

Begg spoke in a low voice from behind him. "I think I do, Ryman. Remember the shooting at French Tony's the other night?"

"Naturally…"

"We all thought you or Zenith were the targets. But we were wrong. You *both* fired at the would-be assailants and killed them, *but they had not been sent to kill you.* You see how jealous Mlle LeVeaux can be. She was still jealous then. Her infatuation at the time, of course, was with you. She did come to see you, didn't she? She needed your help, your expertise. And you needed something only she possessed. The last potent black narcissi. I'd guess it was part of her bargain that Miss Dent should be 'dismissed' – either killed or sent away, that I don't know. When you eventually refused, she decided you were no longer 'partners'. Am I right?"

Ryman was surprised. "You are! But how did you –?"

"Deduction. Simple deduction, my dear fellow, since you are clearly no longer her partner. But she would not be the infamous Voodoo Queen if she were not jealous! Jealousy and passion have informed that evil woman's decisions since she was a girl. Hess and LeGris had sided with you, Ryman, and rebelled against her. So, with a mixture of drugs and hypnotism, she turned them into *zombis* and sent them to French Tony's. To kill the person she believed responsible for your refusal…"

"*Of course!* Molly! She was the target. Molly wanted nothing to do with any of it. But I had to – I had little choice, Begg, believe me."

"I can imagine your predicament. I've seen the drugs over there. The ones you were clearly working on and which Mlle LeVeaux swept to one side. The woman you loved was dying of cancer, and you knew who possessed the means of saving her."

While the Creole woman's attention was on Blasco and the experiment table Ryman answered in a whisper: "Marie had the stuff in its natural state. It's derived from the Amazonian *umboltia*, a species of massive vine which only grows along the upper reaches of the Amazon and Orinoco. It's a form of *curaré*." Ryman's features were drawn, tortured. He was barely able to speak.

"I've read your research, of course. So you discovered what could cure certain forms of cancer – including Miss Dent's."

"Not 'cure', Begg, but inhibit. Essentially you're right. Marie LeVeaux was my only chance. She's an expert on deadly tropical plants. The stuff's never been synthesized. As you know, I have specialized in discovering and developing such serums. It was ironic that when Molly contracted cancer I could only hope to stop the disease spreading by using *curaré* derived from *umboltia*. I got in touch with Marie but she would not give me what she had. She wanted something in return from me." He sighed. "She demanded I use my knowledge to synthesise an antidote to that other kind of *curaré* which simulates death. I made a small amount, but that was all I could produce from the black narcissi she had left. Blasco could not grow an effective plant but possessed the few remaining bulbs. I begged her not to make me her partner, telling her that Molly's life was at stake. She said she would give me what she had – only – only – " Ryman was under considerable strain, his eyes on Molly. "Only she insisted on my keeping that bargain. Not only must I help her synthesise the antidote, I must also contact any desperate acquaintances I'd made in Yarnwell and propose a scheme to them. She would 'kill' them with the deadly *curare* which simulates death – and is death if there is no antidote applied in time – so that they could be restored by the antidote and start a new life somewhere with their share of the insurance. I was desperate, Begg. To save Molly's life meant I had to do something which broke my parole and threatened to make us criminal fugitives again!"

"So you found Marie three men you knew from the race track. Men who needed to fake their own deaths. The unlucky gamblers, Ogg, Price and Tree. They would take out large life insurances which they would then secretly recover from the beneficiaries (all innocent in their case) and pay a large portion to Marie. Through Hess and LeGris she would arrange passports and a change of identity. You believed the agreement over then. But she wanted you to make more antidote and find more 'customers'. You refused. You had already jeopardized yourself."

"That's right, Begg. She believed Molly had persuaded me to go straight. Which was true in part, but – I'd had enough, Begg. I wanted so much to continue with my work on cancers. I was so close to a cure for some of the most invasive kinds, including Molly's!"

Begg saw the desperate truth in Ryman's eyes and was sympathetic. "You were trying to get away with Molly when Mlle Bouvier arrived on the scene…"

Yvette had been listening. She spoke with some difficulty. "I arrived as Ryman was trying to get Molly to their car. They had escaped from the back of the house. I heard shots. When I went to help – well, those foul things of hers, they came pouring out of the doors and overwhelmed me. They took my own gun and knocked me out. When I came to I was hanging here. What does she mean to do with us?"

"This is a continuation of the experiment," said Ryman. "The problem was never how to create a poison. *Curaré* can be very effective. The CL14 strain acts by paralyzing the organs, but otherwise does no other harm. That particular strain does not kill you, whereas most deadly strains work by freezing your lungs so that you effectively drown on dry land! In CL14, however, death is convincingly simulated because this particular strain of the drug produces something more like hibernation in its victims. *But a hibernation which lasts forever!* Or at least until natural processes begin to break down. Effectively, you remain alive, even if you are buried, until you begin to rot. It can take weeks or even years in some cases."

Yvette had turned a little paler. "And the antidote? How does it save you?"

"It counteracts the *curaré* and allows your organs to function normally again. The difficulty, as you heard, is in judging the dosage and duration. It is not yet a science…"

116

"That is why those three 'dead' men came back to life too soon and stumbled out of Jarvis's funeral parlour," said Begg. "Ah! She is indeed a *fiend*!"

"Talk as much as you wish, gentlemen!" Marie's jeering tones came from the other side of the lab. "You have taken the place of the laboratory animals which Ryman kept here. Zenith and I, with Dr Blasco's help, will now complete our experiments! We shall test the antidote on human subjects. Some of course will be brought round too soon, others not soon enough. *Or not at all*. But ultimately we shall determine the dosages we need. Bring out the girl, Molly Dent. She'll be our first subject."

"No! Damn you! No!" As the Voodoo Queen's dead/alive slaves entered the cage Ryman flung himself at them, only to be beaten into semi-consciousness by the hilts of their heavy knives. Molly was cut down and dragged out to where Marie waited. In the Creole's hand was a hypodermic filled with yellow-green liquid.

Zenith shook his head. "A poor subject to begin with. She already has a cocktail of Ryman's serums in her system. How will we know what is active and what is not?"

Marie LeVeaux darted an enquiring glance at Blasco. The little man could scarcely speak from terror but managed to nod his agreement. "Quite right, senorita."

"Put her over there," grated the Voodoo Queen. "Bring another specimen. Oh, look how feeble that one is!" For Molly had fallen to the floor in a dead faint.

"I'm warning you, Marie LeVeaux," shouted Begg. "The police will be here soon enough. I sent my dog for them −"

She laughed harshly. "I saw the dog with your boy. The dog was frightened, like most dogs. It ran away into the woods with its tail between its legs." She gestured with the hypodermic to her slaves and said a few words in Creole.

Yvette's eyes widened. She seemed to come fully awake. "Seaton! Did you come alone? What's happening here? Are the police −?"

Begg shook his head, unable to lie to her. Then he shouted through the bars:

"For Heaven's sake, Zenith! This isn't like you. You were never a coward. You don't make war on innocent women! It's against your whole code!"

Zenith raised a sardonic eyebrow but did not otherwise reply.

Marie was speaking to Professor Blasco. "We only have a small amount of the antidote. The dose we used on the first three was too great. We cannot afford to use too much again. Give them extra *poison*. They are strong specimens. We'll use the other girl."

The *zombis* came back into the cage and, pushing Begg and the others aside, cut Yvette down. She fought with all her skill and courage against them but they easily dragged her out to where Marie LeVeaux waited with her hypodermic. Begg was beside himself, trying to help her. He, too, fought as hard as he could, but the *zombis* were preternaturally strong and easily constrained him.

All eyes were on the drama being played out in the cage. Nobody saw Molly struggle to her feet and stagger to a desk. Barely able to stand, she opened one of the drawers, searching frantically for something she knew to be in there.

Now Marie LeVaux had torn back Yvette's sleeve and signalled for Blasco to prepare a fresh syringe. Trembling, he stabbed the needle into the phial and filled the hypo with *curaré*. Then he took hold of Yvette's arm. Again she began to struggle violently, doing everything she could to stop Blasco from injecting her. But, carefully and slowly, the trembling biologist took the instrument and, urged on by the impatient Voodoo Queen, at last succeeded in injecting Yvette's upper arm!

The young woman continued to fight her captors but her strength was slowly leaving her. Begg knew that if he applied artificial respiration he might save her at that point. She grew red, desperately trying to continue breathing, gasping and clutching at her throat while the 'king and queen of darkness' watched impassively. Blasco, on the other hand, shook with horror and croaked at Zenith and Marie, begging them to stop. Zenith merely chuckled, watching Yvette lose consciousness before the Creole ordered her slaves to drag the detective back into the cage. Next, Baines was manhandled out of the prison and injected in turn. The poor man scarcely made a sound, but there were tears in his eyes as he suddenly crumpled to the floor, almost without trying to breath. Then Ryman, cursing and fighting, was pulled from the cage. "Have you no confidence in your own formula, Dr Ryman? You had better pray you were successful in synthesizing the CL14X — the antidote! Now Professor Blasco! The *curaré*!"

Ryman was a bull. It took him long minutes to succumb and his gradual collapse was not pretty. Begg was forced to turn his head away. Now only Begg and Winker were left.

Realising Zenith and Marie could not be appealed to, Begg had fallen silent, his eyes glaring with impotent fury as the zombis came for Winker, who, brave as always, refused to show fear. Instead he stepped from the cage and removed his own jacket, handing it to one of the zombi-men, for all the world like someone about to take part in an amateur boxing match.

Marie snatched the needle from Blasco's shaking hand, laughing and looking at Begg. "Don't you regret the day you decided to go against me, Mr Seaton Begg?" And with that, she plunged the hypodermic into poor Winker's forearm. Unlike Baines, the young detective fought with all his might to keep from going under, but soon he began to choke and gasp, refusing to show any sign of panic until, like a tall tree felled in a forest, he collapsed straight and noiselessly to the floor.

Now, only Begg was left and he too refused to give his captors any satisfaction. All around him, the others lay prone, succumbed to the *curaré*. The eyes of Blasco, LeVeaux and Zenith were fixed on him as he, too, shook off the grip of the *zombis* and removed his own jacket, baring his arm as Winker had done. He thought he saw a peculiar expression cross Zenith's face, but he said nothing.

Marie LeVeaux was grinning. Her breath was hot on his face and her voice was throaty.

"If this works, we shall know Ryman's formula is right. If not, we shall have to keep experimenting. How does it feel, Mr Begg, to be a laboratory rat? You do not yet know if you can wake from this non-sleep. We will keep testing and testing until we find out whether we have an antidote which works, and then, when we have finished, we shall doubtless get rid of what is left of your bodies and people will never know what became of you. Don't worry. You shall have a proper burial. I thought of digging your grave in a mountain of rubbish – there's a waste-tip not far from here – because, of course, you will still have your senses of smell and hearing. What's more you will probably live far beyond the normal span. You will see, if there is anything to see, before your eyes rot in your head. You will be in suspended animation. A kind of near-immortality. Possibly we shall try some other experiments..."

A terrible sickness came to Begg's stomach as the *curaré* began to take effect. He felt his whole body slowly growing numb. First his feet and hands. Then his head and his legs. Then his arms and now, as his legs buckled beneath him, he found it harder and harder to breath. He gasped, desperately trying to drag air into his lungs, but it was impossible! His head was aching horribly. His eyes would not move and he failed to keep his head up. His legs buckled.

Marie LeVeaux laughed. Her voice seemed to come from a long way off. She brandished another hypodermic. "Of course, there's every chance that this strain of the antidote will not work at all. Perhaps we shall simply give your body to an undertaker. Mr Jarvis, perhaps! Then you'll be buried in utter blackness. You will feel nothing, of course, except the horror, as your body slowly disintegrates and the worms eat your flesh. Only your brain will work. That is the last to go. You will know every detail of what is happening to you!" Her devilish laughter filled those ancient vaults.

And then Begg felt his body losing balance. Moments later, his eyes still open, he fell to the floor, partly on his side so that he could see a little of the laboratory. But, unable to move the smallest muscle, he saw nothing of his friends, only Zenith's sardonic face smiling down at him and Marie LeVeaux wrapping her arms about the Albino and chuckling insanely. He could smell her perfume, the drugs. This, thought Begg, was worse than hell. The truly terrible thing was that he could hear everything. He heard Marie LeVeaux's throaty laughter, Zenith's light, sarcastic voice.

There came a sudden loud report, screams, raised voices. One of those voices was Molly Dent's! *"Bring them back! Bring them back, do you hear!"*

Another shot. The sound of something falling. More agitated voices and Begg felt something wet on his face. He tasted salty blood. Molly's?

Another shot.

BANG!

Zenith's urgent voice: "Quickly! The sooner we do this, the better!"

What was the Albino talking about? What was going on?

"Blasco, you dolt!" called Zenith, urgently. "Get the antidote. And pray Ryman mixed it according to his formula or I will personally inject you with the *curaré* myself."

Blasco's quavering voice: "Ryman? What did he do?"

Begg heard Zenith speak again. "He was ahead of you, you see. While you tried to grow fresh plants from the bulbs of the black narcissus, he attempted scientifically to synthesise the drug it produces! Marie LeVaux used the last of the natural stuff on those three gamblers. It woke them too soon. Now this – this must work! But Ryman distilled so little."

Still Begg could not tell what was happening. He heard Marie Leveaux's voice again. A thud. Another shot.

Then a sudden curse from Zenith. A triumphant shout from Marie LeVeaux. Yet another shot.

Scuffling.

At that moment, Begg would have given a great deal to be able to turn his head. He heard someone gasp – possibly Molly. Then a loud, piercing scream from Marie. "Ah! Ah! Traitor! Help her would you? I should never have trusted you! Your treachery shall not go unpunished, Albino!"

BANG! BANG!

Were the crooks fighting amongst themselves? If so, what weapons were they using?

Suddenly another body slumped over Begg's legs. He could not tell whose it was but something about the smell and feel of the body suggested to him that it was Marie's. And still he could not tell what was going on.

Except he could swear he heard the sound of a police whistle, a door being broken in, a bark he recognized as Stone's and then the gruff familiar voice of Detective Inspector Coutts!

Were they all too late? There was no proven antidote. Begg could not help feeling that the *curare* was going to kill him. Marie LeVeaux had succeeded in her desire for vengeance. He felt the weight lift from his body. She had risen. He heard her shouting at her slaves:

"You shall never have the antidote. *Here is the formula!* There! *I burn it!* Attack! Attack! Kill them all." But her voice was growing feeble. Begg heard metal falling on the flagstones of the laboratory, booted feet hitting those same stones. Then came Zenith's whisper. "Farewell, old enemy. I trust when we meet next it will be upon a more even playing field."

He saw the worried features of Professor Blasco staring into his, heard part of his conversation. "Now we know how to grow the bulbs, but have no more bulbs to grow. Marie LeVeaux took the last ones from the slopes of Pix La Selle, expecting to grow more at the Crystal Palace. But she needed everything she could find just to make a small amount of the natural serum. If Doctor Ryman cannot make a new synthesis, then it's possible that was the last!"

While Begg thought about this, nothing happened, or so it seemed.

The next few hours were to prove extremely frustrating for the detective as first one friendly face and then another came before him. He knew he had been propped in a chair. His head was turned, also, so that he could see Winker, Yvette and Ryman, all evidently in the same position as himself, like so many corpses arranged on seats. But soon feeling began to come back, first in his hands and feet and lastly in his lungs as he drew in a great gasp of cold air.

He heard Ryman explaining something to Coutts. "To analyse the antidote I needed the sap from a black narcissus which grew on the upper slopes of Pix la Selle, the highest mountain in Hayti. Marie had the last plants. Her own and those she stole from Blasco. The stuff's illegal. When not used in conjunction with that particular kind of *curaré*, it's a virulent poison, not unlike the stuff she used to control those zombi-men of hers. Meanwhile she also got me the stuff I needed to treat Molly's cancer. And that was when she increased her price. Of course, I was then in her power. The next thing I knew I was introducing her to those prospective clients for that insurance swindle she'd cooked up. I was no more than a middle man. But believe me, Coutts, I'm not offering you any excuses. I was guilty, right enough. I would have done anything to save Molly."

Coutts answered with gruff emotion. "Well Dr Ryman, I suspect there will be no charges against you. You and Miss Dent seem to have been as much victims of that devil woman as anyone."

Begg saw relief wash over Ryman's features. There was no doubt about his love for Molly Dent. It had made him again a great beneficiary of society.

Something wet wiped Begg's face and he felt like laughing. Stone's great, happy tongue helped him to wake up to normality.

He heard Coutts making another remark and, turning with difficulty, saw him, resting his back against a wall and puffing furiously on his hideous briar. Coutts was addressing Yvette. "You have the landlord to thank for us arriving on time, miss. He telephoned the local police when you hadn't come back for your car. They got in touch with us. We were already down here. We had an odd report that three men, acting rather strangely, were drinking heavily in the Cross Keys without any wherewithal to pay. When the landlord asked for his money, the three 'borrowed' a car and drove away. They weren't in any condition to drive, it seems. They went off the road not far from Yarn Abbey. A terrible smash, I'm afraid. All dead, sadly. Nobody else hurt. Hello, Begg! You've been prone for hours! Why are you grinning like a fool?" Coutts straightened his bowler and glared at the detective.

"Oh, nothing, Coutts. Nothing at all." But Begg saw that Yvette, too, could not help chuckling. "What happened?"

"I just telephoned the yard again. When their next of kin were informed, they said they already *knew* they were dead! Strange, eh? It's becoming a very odd week..." He tipped his bowler still further forward and scratched his head. "I was having a look at the accident when I got the word over our radio car about Miss Yvette's disappearance. I knew Ryman had somehow been mixed up in this business and so I came here with a bunch of brawny lads, just in case. Not that those dead/alive men put up much of a fight once their mistress was finished. Before he left, Zenith seems to have come to the defence of Molly Dent."

"What about those *zombis* she created? Not their fault, you know. She used drugs and hypnotism to control them."

"I know that, Begg, Zenith stuck her with the last hypo! She's still alive but we don't know how to get her back. No antidote left, you see. The *zombis* will be revived and taken back to the docks where they'll be offered jobs."

"But after you heard, how did you find us so quickly, Coutts?" asked Begg. "I thought we were gonners for certain!"

"You were pretty lucky. Old Stone, your bloodhound, led us to the lab. We found him outside barking his head off. When we got here Zenith had already gone to the aid of Molly Dent. From what I could tell, Molly tried to shoot Marie LeVeaux and wounded her. But Marie then went after her with a big knife, giving her a nasty cut, which she'll probably recover from. According to Miss Dent, Zenith sprang to her defence, shooting the Voodoo Queen before we turned up. Between the eyes. Almost his trademark! He's gone now, of course. Zenith rarely stops to have a conversation with the police."

Begg was still somewhat bleary, but he was beginning to understand. In order to rescue Vespa, Zenith had let the Voodoo Queen think he had succumbed to her charms. In saving Vespa he actually he had saved them all, except Beale. Begg said nothing of this to Coutts. After a moment's private thought he said to Ryman: "The antidote worked, then?"

"Evidently it did. That strain of *curaré* isn't rare. CL14 is used for hunting in South America. What *is* hard to make is the antidote. The black narcissus is very rare. Actually it's probably extinct now, in any effective form. Oh, I'll try to synthesise some more but I don't know if I'll have any luck. The natural stuff was my test control. However, the drug I used on Molly to inhibit the growth of her particular cancer is another matter. Molly will probably die of old age before she dies of the disease. That stuff will soon be ready for testing by the BMA."

"What about your antidote they injected into us, Dr Ryman?" asked Winker. "Did it work as she expected?"

"Pretty well, as far as I can tell." Ryman spoke with not a little pride. "But there are likely side effects, I fear."

Sipping a big beaker of tea, Winker showed traces of alarm. "Side effects? What sort of side effects?"

"Well, in my research I found that the serum works *with* the curare to produce a kind of suspended animation in the patient's system. In other words, old age is not 'cured' but slowed down enormously. As, indeed, are many other functions."

"How's that again, doc?" Winker took another sip of the tea Coutts's sergeant had made in Yarn Abbey's kitchens. "You mean if any of us has potential disease, it won't harm us?"

"Not exactly!" Now, Professor Blasco, still looking a little the worse for wear, sat down in a chair across from Begg. "But my brilliant colleague Ryman here, combining CL14 and its antidote, actually managed to inhibit most of the body's ageing processes!"

"It's a side effect we hadn't really thought about." Ryman had begun to laugh at Winker's puzzlement. "The irony is that inadvertently we discovered a 'cure for death'. What mankind's been seeking since it understood it was mortal."

"That stuff makes you immortal?"

"No, but it increases your longevity by quite a bit – maybe to Methuselah lengths! We won't know for certain, of course, because those of us injected with the stuff will need to reach something close to old age before we see how it's effective. The problem is that Marie LeVeaux destroyed my formulae involved in making CL14X. Without a black narcissus, we can't make any more at all. We few are the only ones who have it in our veins! I suspect we'll see the 20th century out and probably the 21st, also."

"Not necessarily something to look forward to," said Yvette with a smile. She turned to Begg. "Oh, my dear, I am so glad you survived. Old Baines, I fear, did not. The strain was too much for his heart."

Begg drew a deep breath. "Poor fellow." Then he said seriously: "But I do not think I would wish to have lived, Yvette, if death had taken you from me."

Whereupon, before the astonished gaze of everyone there, Seaton Begg took Mlle Yvette Bouvier in his arms and kissed her warmly upon her lips.

The Albino's Shadow

George Mann

London, August 1933

I.

"I EVEN HEARD he'd been resurrected from the dead by a blood infusion from some heathen witch doctor. They say he's not even a man any more, but some sort of pale spirit, half ghost, half juju."

Major Absalom rocked back in his seat and fixed Rutherford with a look of absolute sincerity, peering out from beneath his heavy, furrowed brow and bushy eyebrows. He chewed thoughtfully on the end of his pipe, smoke dribbling from his nostrils like the exhalation of a dormant dragon.

Rutherford smiled. He'd always thought the Major was a little too credulous for his own good. "You sound as if you actually believe all these myths about this 'Monsieur Zenith' character," he said, before taking a long draw on his cigarette. He blew the smoke casually from the corner of his mouth, watching his superior officer with interest.

Absalom's frown deepened. His whiskers — which curled impressively from his ears to meet his moustache — twitched as he considered Rutherford's words. "To be truthful with you, Rutherford, I'm not even sure I believe the man himself isn't a myth. I mean, really..." he sighed, leaning forward again and placing both of his palms on the leather surface of his desk.

Rutherford watched him, amused. "I hear the Yard have attributed scores of cases to him over the years. He's one of the most wanted men in the Empire."

Absalom snorted.

"You're not a believer, then, sir?"

"Be that as it may, there are others," Absalom coughed, as if not wishing to give voice to the names themselves, "who do

127

believe he's out there, and moreso, that he's harbouring sinister intentions towards them."

Rutherford stubbed the remains of his cigarette in the cut glass ashtray on Absalom's desk and folded his hands on his lap. "Does the Prime Minister have any evidence to support his claim?"

Absalom raised an eyebrow in surprise. Clearly, he hadn't expected Rutherford to be so well informed. "Of course he doesn't," he said, resignedly. "Simply that he asserts to have received a telephone call from the villain in question."

"And?" Rutherford prompted.

Absalom shrugged. "Only that Monseiur Zenith told him to expect a change in his fortunes."

"It's not a lot to go on," said Rutherford.

"Indeed it's not," agreed Absalom, "and to be honest, if it were anyone else, I should be counselling equanimity. However, we're talking about the Prime Minister. We need to show we're taking it seriously."

Rutherford nodded. "And, of course, rule out the potential of a real threat," he said, smiling.

"Yes, yes, yes," replied Absalom, with bluster. "Goes without saying." He stroked his whiskers absently.

"So you want me to pay a visit to Downing Street, speak with the Prime Minister?" asked Rutherford.

"God, no," said Absalom, grimacing. "Wouldn't want to lumber you with that. I'll take care of the PM." He rocked back in his chair. "No, I want you to look into this Monseiur Zenith character, see if you can't get to the bottom of what's going on. I want to know who he is and what his game is. If," he added, with a roll of his eyes, "he even exists at all, that is."

Rutherford grinned. "I know just where to start," he said.

II.

RUTHERFORD PAUSED FOR a moment at the end of the garden path, chewing on the stub of his cigarette.

The house was just as he remembered it from his visit six months earlier, when he'd called on the professor to interview him regarding the matter of 'the Maharajah's Star'; old, immaculate and somewhat incongruous, nestled as it was amongst its modern counterparts. Not unlike its owner, Rutherford mused with a grin.

The interview had proved successful, but not at all in the manner Rutherford had expected. After hearing Professor Angelchrist's tale, Rutherford had ended up throwing in his lot with the retired agent, helping him to perpetuate a decades-old lie about the whereabouts of an ancient treasure.

It was during the course of the ensuing conversation that Angelchrist had first mentioned 'the albino prince'. It had been only a fleeting reference; a cursory remark to demonstrate another point, but for some reason it had lodged in the back of Rutherford's mind. Now, with hindsight, he realised that Angelchrist could not have been referring to anyone else. It had to be Zenith.

He had no idea whether the professor would know anything more about Rutherford's alabaster-skinned quarry, but regardless, it was the only lead he had. If Angelchrist proved to be a dead end, Rutherford would be forced to go back to Absalom empty-handed.

Rutherford filled his lungs with sharp, sweet tobacco smoke, dropped the stub of the cigarette on the path and crushed it underfoot. He exhaled slowly through the corner of his mouth as he walked towards the door, which — as he'd expected it might — swung open before he'd even had chance to put his boot on the bottom step.

Angelchrist's elderly, bald-headed butler peered out through the narrow crack, a suspicious frown on his face.

"Good afternoon. I'm here to see Professor Angelchrist," said Rutherford, genially.

The man's expression altered almost immediately as he seemed to recognise Rutherford's voice. "I fear I did not recognise you for a moment, Mr. Rutherford. I do beg your pardon." The door opened fully and the butler gave a slight smile as he beckoned Rutherford into the house

Rutherford smiled. "I imagine the professor receives a great many visitors," he said. "You couldn't possibly be expected to remember them all."

"No, sir," said the butler in a droll voice. "It was the...well, it was the hat."

Rutherford couldn't help but laugh at the butler's derisory tone. He reached up and removed the offending item – a wide-brimmed fedora he had purchased in New York a few years earlier – and handed it to the other man as he stepped over the threshold, ducking his head beneath the low beam.

The butler took the hat without further comment, closing the door behind them and following Rutherford into the house. He placed it carefully on a nearby hat stand and held out his arm for Rutherford's overcoat.

The hallway was shrouded in darkness, and Rutherford could hear the groaning and ticking of myriad clockwork machines in the shadowy recesses. A large, potted aspidistra stood at the foot of the staircase, and a wooden, life-sized figure of a caveman loomed down eerily from the landing above.

Rutherford had a sense that the house was crowded with the accumulated detritus of decades, paraphernalia of a thousand long-forgotten adventures. He longed to explore, to go rummaging and digging amongst all of this wondrous stuff, to unpick the tales attached to each item.

"If you'd like to come this way, sir," said the butler, interrupting his reverie, "I'm sure the professor will be delighted to speak with you."

Rutherford nodded, and followed behind the other man as he led them through the winding bowels of the house, past the propped up case of an Egyptian mummy, a strange looking contraption labelled the 'aetheric calibrator' and a display case filled with primitive effigies and dolls. Atop this display case sat a large brass owl, which turned its head to follow them as they passed, clacking its metallic wings and chirruping noisily.

"Ignore the owl, sir," said the butler, "it has eyes only for the lacquered furniture, damnable thing."

Rutherford tried not to laugh.

A moment later, the butler stopped abruptly outside a panelled door, and rapped loudly three times. He turned the handle and pushed the door open for Rutherford. "In here, Mr. Rutherford," he said, shooing Rutherford in. "You make yourself comfortable, and I'll organise some tea."

"Thank, you," said Rutherford, realizing for the first time that he didn't actually know the butler's name. He stepped over the threshold into the dimly lit room beyond.

Professor Angelchrist was sitting in a chair by the fire. He might not have moved in the intervening six months since Rutherford's previous call – he sat in precisely the same position, a book balanced neatly upon his lap. He looked up when Rutherford came into the room, and smiled warmly. "Welcome back, Mr. Rutherford. It's good to see you again."

"Likewise," said Rutherford, crossing the room to shake Angelchrist by the hand.

"Please, take a seat, and tell me how I might be of assistance to you," said Angelchrist, waving Rutherford to the chair opposite. "Is it with regards to the Maharajah's Star?"

"In a manner of speaking," replied Rutherford, settling into his seat. "I remember that, during my previous visit, you told me of an albino prince from Eastern Europe who'd been searching for the Star."

"Ah, yes. Monsieur Zenith," said Angelchrist, with a tight smile. "What an interesting fellow."

"So he's real, then?" asked Rutherford, sensing a story.

Angelchrist laughed. "Oh, yes, Mr. Rutherford, as real as you or I." He folded his book shut and placed it neatly on the side table. "I met him, once," he continued. "He came here but a week after you, searching for the Star."

Rutherford couldn't hide the surprise on his face. "He came here?"

Angelchrist laughed again. "Indeed. He was quite charming, in his own way. Resourceful, too. He'd followed the trail of the Star and, like you, Mr. Rutherford, he'd established that I was the last person to see it before it disappeared. He came here to ask me for it."

Rutherford blanched. "Did he threaten you, professor?"

Angelchrist chuckled. "Oh, no. Not at all. He was a perfect gentleman. When he discovered the truth about the Star, he was most amused. He seemed to have an appreciation for the irony of the situation. He stayed for a while, telling me something of his exploits, of his long search for the Star, and then left without further ado."

Rutherford frowned. This didn't sound like the behavior of a hardened criminal. "Did he leave you a calling card or a forwarding address? I've been tasked with finding him. A threat has been made, you see, and it seems likely that Monsieur Zenith may be behind it."

Angelchrist shook his head. "This was some months ago now, Mr. Rutherford. A man like Monsieur Zenith does not stay still for long," he replied.

"Nevertheless...do you have any notion of where I might find him?"

Angelchrist shook his head. "I fear not."

Rutherford gave a resigned sigh. "Then I thank you for your help, Professor. You've been most helpful." He stood, brushing himself down. "I suspected I was hoping for too much that you might be able to put me on the albino's trail."

Angelchrist chuckled. "Ah, now I didn't say that, Mr. Rutherford. If you want to find Monsieur Zenith, then there's someone I think you should talk with."

Rutherford dropped back into his seat, intrigued. "Who?"

"Miss Veronica Hobbes," said Angelchrist.

"Miss Veronica Hobbes?" echoed Rutherford, surprised.

"Indeed. Miss Hobbes has, over the years, had cause to pit her wits against Monsieur Zenith on a number of occasions," said Angelchrist.

"Alongside Sir Maurice Newbury?" asked Rutherford.

"And alone," replied Angelchrist, nodding. "If there's anyone I know who could assist you in this matter, it's Miss Hobbes."

Rutherford grinned. "Do you know how to reach her?"

"Indeed I do, Mr. Rutherford," said Angelchrist, heaving himself up out of his chair with a groan. "You wait here for Casper to bring the tea, and I shall make a telephone call."

III.

THEY MET AT a restaurant in Kensington, sitting by the window in the shadow of a broad awning. It was a brisk morning and Rutherford would have preferred to sit inside, but the lady seemed intent on sitting out. She sipped at her Earl Grey and watched him over the brim of the teacup, seemingly impervious to the cold.

He watched her in turn, as if they were circling opponents, sizing each other up. After a moment, she spoke. "Well, Mr. Rutherford?"

He was about to answer when the waiter bustled over and began describing the specials with great bonhomie. Rutherford found none of the proposed delicacies fired his imagination, so ordered a simple salad, and only then so as not to seem impolite. In truth, he would have been happy to subsist on nothing but strong coffee and cigarettes.

The waiter hurried off again and the woman — Miss Veronica Hobbes — waited patiently as Rutherford slowly extracted a cigarette from his silver tin, lit it with a match and took a long, welcome draw.

She was not at all what he'd been expecting. He wasn't sure what he had been expecting, but it hadn't been this. He supposed he'd imagined she'd seem older, more like Angelchrist, a relic of a bygone age.

In fact, she was far younger than Angelchrist, and although she was in her early fifties, she had the look of an attractive woman ten years her junior. Her hair did not yet show signs of turning to grey, remaining a dark, voluminous brown, and aside from a tiny, sickle-shaped scar on her left cheek, her skin was unlined and unblemished. Her eyes were striking and full of life and energy.

Strangely, Rutherford thought he could hear a faint ticking sound as he leaned closer to her across the table, as if she were harbouring a small carriage clock in her handbag. He decided it would be impolite to enquire.

"Thank you for coming," he said, sincerely. "I imagine you know who I represent?"

She smiled knowingly and took another sip of her tea. "I know that you work for the secret service, if that's what you mean?" she said, quietly, so that they might not be overheard. "I know that you're on the trail of the albino prince, and that you don't have any idea of where to begin, or whether he even actually exists at all."

Rutherford laughed. "Yes," he confirmed, "That's about the size of it, Miss Hobbes." She was clearly more informed than he'd anticipated, too. He made a mental note not to underestimate this striking woman. "Although Professor Angelchrist assures me as to the corporeal nature of the villain," he added.

Miss Hobbes smiled and placed her teacup gently on its saucer. "Oh, he exists, Mr. Rutherford. I can very much attest to that."

Rutherford blew smoke from the corner of his mouth, watching as it was quickly dispersed on the frigid breeze. "The professor mentioned you'd had occasion to go up against Monsieur Zenith during your time in active service?"

Miss Hobbes laughed, and her face lit up in amusement. "He does have a way with understatement," she said.

"Indeed?" prompted Rutherford.

She sighed, indulgently. "One does not simply trifle with Zenith, Mr. Rutherford. To him it's all a game, you see? All of it. He revels in the tete-a-tete. Once you engage, it becomes a battle of wits, a game of chess, played out across many years and many continents."

"And you, Miss Hobbes — you entered into this game with the albino?"

"I had little choice. Our paths crossed during an investigation, and he became...intrigued by me. In the years following the war, barely a month would go by without our meeting once again. His criminal activities were diverse and reckless, but never, ever, boring. Stolen works of art, voodoo cults, ancient curses, flesh golems and clockwork shop dummies — just a few of the nefarious schemes to which I found myself in opposition." Miss Hobbes paused as the waiter delivered her sandwich to the table. "Another pot of tea, please, waiter," she said, with a smile. "Earl Grey." She glanced at Rutherford. "I've developed something of a taste for it. It's all Maurice will ever drink."

Rutherford laughed. "And how did Sir Maurice feel about all of this attention you received from Monsieur Zenith?"

Miss Hobbes raised a single eyebrow. "Oh, Zenith was only ever interested in the game, Mr. Rutherford. I just happened to be another of the players." She picked at her sandwich. "Over time, his interest waned. Perhaps I became predictable, too easy to anticipate? Now, I believe, he has engaged another playmate. Nevertheless, I often wonder if, perhaps one day, I shall hear from him again."

"I thought you had retired, Miss Hobbes?" said Rutherford.

"People like us never retire, Mr. Rutherford. We simply grow older, and slow down." She smiled. "Here comes your salad."

Rutherford stubbed out the remains of his cigarette as the waiter placed the plate on the table.

"I need to find him, Miss Hobbes," he said, once they were alone again.

"Yes, I daresay the Prime Minister has suffered a few sleepless nights of late," said Miss Hobbes, wryly.

Rutherford grinned, despite himself. "Yes, I daresay he has."

"I fear Monsieur Zenith is a wily devil, Mr. Rutherford. He shall not be easy to find."

"I don't doubt it, Miss Hobbes. But do you know where I can even begin my search? You mentioned that Zenith has engaged another in his games."

Miss Hobbes grinned. "Indeed. There's a man, a detective, who lives on Baker Street." She reached for her handbag. "Let me give you his address."

IV.

THE DETECTIVE RECLINED in his chair and regarded Rutherford appraisingly. He was handsome, with a square set jaw, fine dark hair swept back from his forehead and the solid-looking physique of a boxer. He was dressed in an unassuming black suit, the collar left open while he relaxed by the fire. Rutherford felt a little uncomfortable beneath his penetrating gaze, but was nevertheless drawn to the man, who — he'd decided — was harbouring a fierce intelligence behind his piercing blue eyes.

A large bloodhound was curled up by his feet, and his housekeeper — a bumbling, rotund woman whose propensity for malapropisms, even in the scant few moments in which Rutherford had met her, seemed utterly at odds with the calm sophistication of her employer — was making tea.

He'd come here directly following his meeting with Miss Hobbes, on the off chance that he'd find the detective at home, and much to his surprise he'd been admitted and ushered into the detective's consulting room. He sat there now, before the dying embers of a warming fire, studying the detective's face for any signs of a reaction. He had, moments earlier, imparted the news of Monsieur Zenith's threat to the Prime Minister.

"Zenith is a dangerous foe indeed, Mr. Rutherford. You should watch your step," said the detective, folding his hands upon his lap. He was wearing a thoughtful expression.

Rutherford smiled. "I'm sure I've faced worse," he replied, without humour.

The detective shook his head. "I sincerely doubt that, Mr. Rutherford. Zenith is dangerous because he cares little for his own existence. He lives only for the thrill of the chase. To him, all of this — life, criminality, danger — is a game. A game he insists he will win, at any cost, even his own life."

"You make him sound utterly insane," said Rutherford, weighing up the detective's words. They seemed to chime with the opinions expressed by Miss Hobbes earlier that morning. The portrait he was assembling of this albino prince was one of a deranged genius, intent on finding an exciting way in which to die.

"Not insane," replied the detective. "Simply bored. Weary of this world, and looking to fill his hours with excitement. He craves those things most others fear. He commits his crimes not for political or penury gain, but because he is searching for distraction, for thrills. When he is not being tested in such a way, he succumbs to a fatalistic state of ennui, and gives himself over to his favoured intoxication, opium."

"He's an opium eater?" asked Rutherford, surprised.

"Indeed. A most voracious one, at that," replied the detective. "But do not let that fool you, Mr. Rutherford. He is at his most dangerous when his mind is not distracted. That's when he cooks up his most diabolical schemes, his most dangerous endeavors. He will look to push himself ever closer to the precipice, raising the stakes, and in turn, the reward. The greater the danger, the bigger the thrill."

"You've faced him many times before?" asked Rutherford.

The detective laughed. "Oh yes, Mr. Rutherford. On countless occasions. He might have killed me more than once, save for his unusual moral code and his desire not to forgo a worthy opponent. Zenith obeys only his own rules, and they are close to unfathomable."

"I see that I have my work cut out," said Rutherford, with a sigh. "But tell me, do you think he's serious?"

"In his threat to the Prime Minister?" The detective paused, and then his shoulders heaved in a resigned shrug. "Impossible to say. I find it hard to imagine what he could possibly hope to gain from such an undertaking, other than sheer amusement. I doubt he'll be considering murder — although he certainly has before. No, I imagine his scheme will be to somehow discredit the Prime Minister and force a resignation. Assuming, of course, that he even has anything on the man. It wouldn't be unlike Zenith to fake a controversy just to stir things up a little." The detective smiled wistfully.

"You sound as if you almost admire him," said Rutherford.

"Oh, I do, Mr. Rutherford. In many ways. Yet in others I find him utterly despicable. I will, when the opportunity arises, take every measure to see him locked behind bars. My moral code is not as complex as the albino's, and while I recognise and perhaps even appreciate his genius, I still see, nevertheless, a criminal mind at work. One day he will overreach, and I will be there to catch him when he falls."

"You'll help me, then?" asked Rutherford. "You'll assist me in locating Monsieur Zenith and bringing this threat against the Prime Minister to an end?"

The detective sighed. "Alas, Mr. Rutherford, I find myself entangled with a prior engagement, and one of equal importance to the security of the realm. The Master Mummer is once more afoot in London, and I'm working with the Yard to put a stop to his schemes. We believe he intends to cause a train to derail as it pulls into King's Cross Station, and to use the ensuing panic as cover for a transaction of some sort. As yet, we're not entirely sure as to the nature of that transaction, but I have a fear he's looking to smuggle one of his associates into the capital as part of some even bolder strategy." The detective met Rutherford's gaze. "Even now, the Yard is working to ascertain which train has been sabotaged and targeted. I may be called upon at any moment."

Rutherford nodded. "I quite understand," he said. "Your dedication to the protection of the nation does you credit. I see that your reputation is well earned."

The detective chuckled. "Perhaps." He reached for his briar pipe, which was resting on the arm of his chair. He watched Rutherford in silence for a moment. "I fear you are not yet fully aware of the danger you are facing, Mr. Rutherford. Once you engage Zenith, you will be unable to disentangle yourself from his web. You will find yourself in the midst of a battle of wits, from which the only way out is to win. Unless, of course, he grows tired of you and sees to it that you are dead."

For the first time, Rutherford realised that the detective was actually afraid of the albino. He felt suddenly cold. "Nevertheless, I cannot put my own safety above that of the Prime Minister," said Rutherford, steadfastly. "I have a job to do."

The detective nodded, sucking on his pipe. "Very well, Mr. Rutherford. I shall tell you what you need to know. As I explained, Zenith is a consummate opium eater. He keeps a Japanese manservant known as Oyani, and it is this man whom he charges with the maintenance of his addiction. Oyani will need a regular supply of the drug for his master. Therefore, if you wish to find Zenith, you need only look for the Japanese."

Rutherford smiled. He was sure the detective was making it sound simpler than it was, but this – finally – was the lead he'd been searching for. "My thanks to you," he said.

"Don't thank me yet," said the detective, quietly. "In time you may feel quite differently about the matter."

Rutherford sighed. He'd have to cross that bridge, he decided, when he came to it.

V.

IT HAD TAKEN him three days to find the Japanese, three days during which there had been no more threats made to the Prime Minister via his private telephone line, but throughout which the politician had continued to press Major Absalom for any sign of progress.

Ever the diplomat, Absalom had assured the Prime Minister that Rutherford was on the trail of the villain, and that the matter would soon be brought to a close. The Major had then telephoned Rutherford in the dead of night to unleash his own barrage of threats, berating him for his failure to locate the man whom Absalom himself considered to be nothing more than a myth. As Rutherford had discovered, however, his superior did not take kindly to being reminded of this fact, which, of course, he now deemed to be utterly inconsequential.

Thankfully the newspapers were yet to get hold of the story, and so it only remained — so Absalom had put it — for Rutherford to bring the matter to a swift conclusion. Locating Zenith had now become Rutherford's sole aim. He had barely been home in the last week, and he could feel the pressure of the situation bearing down on him like a pressing weight upon his shoulders. He could almost sense Absalom's whiskered presence looming over his shoulder, watching him as he worked.

Equally thankfully, the detective's steer had proved to be a good one, although the consequent tour of London's less than salubrious establishments of intoxication — the Chinese operated opium dens — had been a taxing and largely unrewarding business. Rutherford's questions had led him to become embroiled in two brawls, and at least one attempt had been made on his life as he'd lounged on a divan in a place called 'Johnny Chang's', pretending to be lost in an opium dream while in fact keeping a watchful eye on the comings and goings of the clientele. The would-be assassin had been nothing but a child – a Chinese boy in the employ of the owners of the house, charged with despatching any unwanted visitors and making off with their wallets. Rutherford had shown the boy the back of his hand, before making a swift exit from the establishment in question.

Finally, however, the net was closing on Monsieur Zenith. From where he now sat, lounging upon a daybed in the semi-darkness and beneath a fog of thick, sweet-smelling smoke, Rutherford could see the little Japanese manservant deep in conversation with one of the Chinese attendants. If Oyani knew he was being watched he gave no outward sign of it, continuing with his master's business – the procurement of a new supply of opium – quite readily.

Rutherford had been forced to make a pact with the devil in order to secure this trap. The owner of the house – Meng Li – was one of the most notorious Chinese crime lords in the Empire, and his men had identified Rutherford as an agent within minutes of him entering the iniquitous den. This, in itself, had not surprised Rutherford, but the fact that Meng Li himself had chosen to pay him a visit was more cause for astonishment. Not only that, but the man had seemed to know all about Rutherford's search for the Japanese manservant of Monsieur Zenith.

"You search for Oyani, whose master is the white ghost, he of pale flesh and crimson eyes," Meng Li had said, standing over Rutherford as he reclined on the daybed, feigning delirium. To Rutherford the crime lord himself had appeared somewhat wraith-like, with sunken eyes, jaundiced skin and a long, dripping moustache and beard. His flowing silken robes skimmed the floor as he moved, giving the impression he was floating on a carpet of billowing opium smoke. It was impossible to discern his age from his appearance, but his voice spoke of untold decades, perhaps longer.

"I do," Rutherford had responded, knowing that lying to this man was in no way an option. He would have been dead before he had finished his sentence.

"Then I can help you, Mr. Rutherford, in your quest," Meng Li had continued, with a smile, "for a price."

"Name it," Rutherford had said, perhaps even then knowing that he was involving himself in something decidedly inadvisable.

"Only that I may call upon you, Mr. Rutherford, if I should find myself with need to," Meng Li had said, in a tone so reasonable that Rutherford had almost missed his meaning. An eye-for-an-eye. If he chose to accept this man's help, he would be in his debt. That, in itself, might prove to be deadly. But what choice had he had?

"I accept your offer," Rutherford had replied, with a bow of his head.

"Very wise, Mr. Rutherford. The hand of Meng Li, once extended, is not to be shunned," the crime lord had said, with a broad grin. "Now, let us speak of Oyani."

So it was that Rutherford had been granted leave to lay in wait for the manservant for what transpired to be his daily visit to the opium den. Now, only a few hours later, he watched as Oyani concluded his business, slipping the small package of opium into the folds of his coat and handing over a sheaf of notes.

Rutherford made ready to follow him, gathering his coat and checking his revolver in his pocket. With luck, the Japanese would finally lead him to Zenith.

As yet, Rutherford had no idea what he would do when he found him.

VI.

OYANI HAD TRAVELLED on foot, and as such had proved relatively easy to trail. He'd made little attempt at concealment, and Rutherford had kept to the shadows, keeping pace with the manservant, but at enough of a distance that Oyani would not – he hoped – become aware of his presence.

They had crossed town for at least two miles before arriving at St. John's Wood, ducking down unfamiliar side streets and alleyways, at one point taking a short cut across a small, leafy park.

Eventually, Oyani had come to a stop before a large Georgian building that bore the legend: BROUGHAM MANSIONS on a small, brass plaque. It was an impressive edifice that had clearly once been the home of a well-to-do sophisticate, but had now been broken up into a series of luxury apartments. Zenith, Rutherford considered, must have taken up temporary residence in one such apartment.

Rutherford watched from behind a tree on the other side of the road as Oyani dug around in his pocket for a key, slipped it into the lock and opened the door to the foyer. He disappeared inside.

Moments passed. Rutherford hesitated, trying to decide on the best course of action, and then, just as he was about to step out from behind the boughs of the great oak, Oyani appeared once again in the doorway. The manservent glanced from side to side, shrugged, and then announced, loudly to the street at large: "Won't you come in, Mr. Rutherford? You are, after all, expected."

Rutherford bristled with shock. Expected? But...how did Oyani know Rutherford's name? Or that he'd been followed here? Had the Chinese attendant tipped the manservant off, back in the opium den? Rutherford tried to think on his feet. What should he do?

"Monsieur Zenith awaits you in the drawing room," said Oyani, and Rutherford knew, then, that he had been outplayed. The game had already begun, and Rutherford was already one move behind.

He took a deep breath, forcing himself to remain calm and level-headed. He stepped out from behind the tree. "Thank you, Oyani," he said, with a smile. "Tell your master I should be only too pleased to join him."

Oyani bowed, and then disappeared inside once more, leaving the door hanging open for Rutherford.

So, this was it. Behind that door was the man he had heard so much about, the man who had threatened the Prime Minister, and who many – including the head of the Secret Service – believed to be nothing more than a phantom, a ridiculous myth. Rutherford knew now, beyond a shadow of a doubt that he was dealing with a man of absolute genius, a master manipulator; a man so adept at managing his reputation that he'd been able to construct an entire mythology around his very existence.

Rutherford took a deep breath, and then set out to meet him.

As he crossed the road and approached the door, he became aware of the strains of a violin emanating from one of the first floor apartments, a soulful lament, played by an exceptional hand. He followed the sound, through the grandiose entrance hall, up the immense central staircase and toward an open door that led into one of the apartments. Steeling himself, he stepped inside.

Oyani was waiting to greet him, and wordlessly ushered him on into the drawing room. He slipped his hand into his pocket, feeling the comforting butt of his revolver against his palm.

The room was dressed after the appearance of its owner: in swathes of ebony and startling white. The floor was laid in a chequerboard of alternating black and white marble, whilst the walls were washed in brilliant white paint. Black drapes hung across the window, and a low divan sat in the centre of the room, covered in a crimson throw. A tall, gilt-framed mirror hung above the fireplace, in which leaping flames licked gently at a wooden log.

Monsieur Zenith himself stood with his back to Rutherford, dressed from collar to toe in immaculate black, his right arm

143

moving slowly back and forth with the ebb and tide of the strains of his violin.

Rutherford sensed the door closing behind him as Oyani retreated, leaving him alone in the room with the albino.

"Don't you think it's sublime how a simple phrase on the violin can describe such exquisite pain?" said Zenith, his voice a low, epicurean drawl.

Rutherford remained silent, studying Monsieur Zenith's back. His grip tightened on the revolver in his pocket. After a moment, the violin playing ceased.

"Oh, do put the gun down, Mr. Rutherford. You shan't be needing it," said the albino, pompously. "I should consider it very bad manners indeed if you were to shoot me on our first date." He turned then, glancing back over his shoulder, and Rutherford was granted his first proper glance at the albino's face.

He was stunningly handsome, with a profile that might have been hewn from the purest Cararra marble. His thin, sensuous lips were drawn in a tight smile, and his eyes were orbs of the deepest crimson. His white hair was short and swept back from his forehead, and he was dressed in pristine evening wear – a black suit and velvet cape, with a red silk cravat – even at this time in the mid-afternoon.

"I'm here – "

"I know why you're here," said Zenith, cutting him off abruptly. He lowered his violin and bow, placing them on a lacquered sideboard before turning and crossing the room. He flicked his cape out behind him and dropped onto the divan, stretching out like a supine cat. At no point did his gaze leave Rutherford's face. "But let's not talk of such prosaic matters, Mr. Rutherford. Let us get to know each other a little, first of all."

Rutherford sighed, withdrawing his hand from his pocket. He glanced behind him, located a high-backed chair and dropped into it. "You cast a long shadow, Monsieur Zenith," said Rutherford, calmly.

"For one so pale?" replied Zenith, wryly. "Yes, I understand you've heard the testimony of a number of my acquaintances. And yet still you came. I find this...most satisfactory."

Rutherford must have frowned, because Zenith allowed himself an amused smile.

"Am I not everything you expected, Mr. Rutherford? Do I disappoint?"

Rutherford hardly knew how to respond. "I have yet to form a full and proper opinion, Monsieur," he replied, levelly.

Zenith laughed, and his long eyelashes flickered. "Quite so. I do enjoy it when people are honest with one another. Don't you? Saves all that ridiculous posturing."

"Then allow me to ask you an honest question, Monsieur."

"Be my guest."

"Why? Why threaten the Prime Minister?"

"Oh, this again," said Zenith, waving his hand and affecting an air of disinterest. "Why not?" he said, in response.

"But what could you possibly hope to gain? Was it blackmail you had in mind?"

"Nothing so prosaic, Mr. Rutherford." Zenith looked him in the eye. "If we're still being honest with one another, perhaps it's time I confessed. I never had any intention of seeing it through. The threat to the Prime Minister was a bluff, a flippant sham, a fake." He laughed. "Does that surprise you?"

"No," said Rutherford. "No, it doesn't surprise me. But it nevertheless intrigues me. I still wish to know why."

Zenith smiled again. "Excellent. I see, Mr. Rutherford that you shall do quite well."

Rutherford felt his heart skip a beat. "I beg your pardon?"

"I'm bored, Mr. Rutherford. Peter. I can call you Peter?" Rutherford nodded his assent. "My detective friend is otherwise engaged, and I find myself in need of...company."

"You have Oyani," said Rutherford.

"Ah, but I require a very particular sort of company, Peter. You see – this world, I find, is a dreary place, when all is said and done. I need a companion who can offer a diversion, a distraction from the tiresome, day-to-day business of living."

"A plaything, you mean?" asked Rutherford, harshly.

"Not at all," said Zenith, with a conciliatory tone. "That's quite the point. Rather someone who might offer up a challenge, who might present at least a modicum of intelligence."

"So...your scheme, the reason for your threatening telephone call to the Prime Minister – it was all to draw someone out, bait for a new opponent for your infernal games?"

Zenith sighed contentedly. "And you answered the call with perfect aplomb."

Rutherford swallowed. His mouth was dry. So all of this – all of those conversations with Angelchrist, Miss Hobbes and the detective, his parlay with Meng Li – all of it had been a kind of extended job interview, a test by which Zenith might identify his latest opponent in the grand game of his life. By finding him, by following Oyani here, Rutherford had effectively volunteered himself for the position. "What if I do not agree to this risible business?" he asked.

"Then, of course, your precious Prime Minister will find his darkest secrets spread across the evening headlines."

"So I'm to become a sacrificial lamb?"

"Oh, don't look at it like that, Peter. We'll have fun, you and I. Two kings commanding our legions of knights and pawns, each trying to stay one step ahead of the other." Zenith swung his legs down from the divan, pulling himself up into a sitting position. "So, Peter. Do we have an understanding?"

"I don't see that I have any choice," said Rutherford, resignedly. "Unless, of course, I reach for my revolver and shoot you now."

Zenith scowled. "I should hope you would not prove so uncouth," he said, standing. "You'd make a terrible mess of the décor."

Rutherford laughed. In spite of everything, he was strangely attracted to this most unusual of criminals. "We have an understanding, then," he said. "The Prime Minister will rest easily tonight."

"Oh, I shouldn't have thought so," said Zenith. "Not knowing the sorts of thing he gets up to after nightfall."

The door opened, and Rutherford turned to see Oyani waiting in the hallway to show him out.

"Until we meet again, then, Peter," said Zenith, extending his hand. Rutherford took it and held it for a moment. It was surprisingly warm.

"Good day, Monsieur Zenith," he said, and then turned and followed Oyani to the door.

VII.

THE RED TELEPHONE box stood like a bright sentinel on the street corner, the herald of a new age. Rutherford smiled to himself as he opened the door and stepped inside, regarding the primitive machinery before him, all dials and coiled cabling. He'd spent time in New York a few years earlier – during the height of the cold war – and the holotube technology the Americans had developed quite outstripped the more traditional telephony system still in place across England. Nevertheless, it would suffice for his needs.

He lifted the receiver to his ear. "Operator? Yes, Whitehall 1212, please. Thank you."

The telephone buzzed at the other end. After a moment, it clicked, and a woman's voice spoke on the other end. "Yes?"

"Hello, Ginny. It's Peter. I need to speak with Absalom," he said. The woman was Absalom's secretary, Ginny Roberts.

A pause. And then: "I'm afraid he's busy, Peter. In with the PM. He's not accepting calls."

"He'll want to accept this one, Ginny. Trust me."

"Sorry Peter. No can do." She sighed. "You know how he is," she said, apologetically.

"Very well. Can you give him a message for me, then?"

"Of course."

"Can you tell him the threat to the PM has been eliminated?"

"Yes. I'll tell him right away." She paused again. "Is everything quite well, Peter?"

"Yes, everything's fine, Ginny. Don't worry. Just pass on the message for me, if you will."

"Yes, I will. 'The threat to the PM has been eliminated'," she parroted. "Good job, Peter."

"Thank you, Ginny. See you later?"

"Not tonight, Peter. I'm off early for the weekend. Going dancing with Evie."

Rutherford laughed at the sheer normality of it all. "Well, you have a good time, Ginny. Watch out for yourself.

"Goodbye, Peter."

"Goodbye." He replaced the receiver and leaned back against the inside of the telephone box. His heart was hammering frantically in his chest. It was over. The job was done. The Prime Minister could sleep safely in his bed.

For Rutherford, however, it was only just beginning. The game was afoot, and he had no idea when, or how, Zenith would make the next move. The strange thing was...he actually found himself relishing the idea. The notion of meeting with such a remarkable character again filled him with a thrill of anticipation. He remembered the words of Miss Veronica Hobbes, spoken in the restaurant just a few days earlier: "His criminal activities were diverse and reckless, but never, ever, boring."

To Rutherford, there was promise in those words.

Rutherford pushed open the door of the telephone box and stepped out into the brisk afternoon. He turned his collar up against the chill, and started off down the road. He would catch a cab back to Whitehall, where he'd offer Absalom just enough of the facts to put the major's mind at rest.

Then, he decided, he might see about a game of chess at his club. After all, he was going to have to get some practice.

148

Zenith's End

Stuart Douglas

I.

THROUGHOUT MY LONG life, my most immediate problem has always been boredom, which deplorable yet apparently inexorable condition has plagued me more and more with each passing year.

The dawning of the nineteen-seventies promised no relief, so far as I could see.

As I closed the door of the waiting taxicab behind me and gestured for the driver to take me back to my hotel, I took one final look at what had once been the home of the man I had been pleased to call my nemesis. Baker Street looked empty and grey in the winter rain, and more than ever I was aware that my time had passed. He was gone, and had by all accounts had spent his last years in enterprises which would once have been far below him, grubbing about amongst the lowest sort of people, reduced to catching small criminals in smaller crimes. The maid who answered the door of his former home had simply said that he had gone away and that his replacement, a Dr Winton, was not at home.

Perhaps it was for the best, however. I could not be sure of the welcome I would receive, after all. More importantly to me, I retained the aspect and physique of a young man, even if my mind was older than the century itself, while he must be an elderly and decrepit husk – and in such a circumstance there is no honour in either challenge or victory. Like so many other things I had seen since returning from the East, my rivalry with the man was at an end. Perhaps if he too had taken Manchu's potion we might have continued our battle indefinitely, but only I had had the nerve (though, if truth be told, I doubt he would have been interested) and thus only I may remain young forever.

Even now, half a century later, I can close my eyes and see the little chinaman beckoning me through a beaded curtain, into his master's inner sanctum. The smell of opium and hashish was thick in the air and somewhere outside I could hear a girl singing, shrilly but not unpleasantly. A clock ticked nearby, and those sounds have stayed with me for fifty years, the clock a metronome measuring the passage of the girl's tune and my own footsteps as I followed the chinese across the stone floor.

Manchu was taller than I expected, but he radiated a menace that even I had to respect. He raised a hand and if I now imagine his fingernails to have been as long and sharp and curved as scimitars, well it has been a long time and the room *was* filled with opium smoke. In any case, he uncurled those bladelike nails like a flytrap plant, exposing a tiny jade box on his palm. 'You have it, Monsieur Zenith?' he said and I nodded. It matters not what I had or to what use Manchu later put it – by now everyone involved but myself is dead and the deeds themselves have crumbled like dust and gone unremembered – but it was enough, and I left the den of Manchu with the box in my pocket.

All that long night I hesitated – not from fear, for of all things death is the one I fear least. But I was unsure whether I wanted the prize I had laboured so long and hard to attain. Often I find this to be case. The pleasure is in the act of obtaining a treasure, not in the treasure itself. Eternal youth is a temptation, no doubt, but one which I might in due course regret. Everyone I knew would age while I remained young; would die while I remained living. To be young forever might also mean to be alone forever.

I took the elixir, nonetheless.

The sound of knocking brought me back to the present day. The driver of the taxicab was rapping with his knuckles on the divider, alerting me to the fact that we had arrived back at my hotel. I reached forward to pay the man and caught a glimpse of my own reflection in the dividing glass. Dark sunglasses covered my sensitive pink eyes, even on a wet and cloudy London day, and a cream hat hid my white hair. The top half of a crushed linen suit was also visible and it struck me that I too was not what I once had been. Like London itself, I was far reduced from my prime; we had both become dusty and grey, the old city and the old man, and the efforts we made to retain a youthful appearance increasingly failed to fool anyone. Everything had become more ugly and more commonplace – even I. To my surprise it turned out that it took only a handful of decades to exhaust the world of both challenges and novelties. It had, in fact, turned out to be a far smaller and more mundane place than I had thought. This visit to England (my first in forty years) had served merely to make concrete what I had long suspected. It was time for an end to Monsieur Zenith.

Freshly resolved, I pulled my cigarette case from my pocket. Inside lay half a dozen of my special tiny cigarettes. Five of these were laced with opium, that enveloping drug which casts a soft blanket around me, making the world more palatable for a while. The other, marked with a thin gold paper band, contained only swift and painless death. I tipped them all into my palm and with my thumbnail flicked the paper band to the floor of the taxicab. I rolled the cigarettes around in my hand for a second then replaced them in the case. Now not even I knew which would kill, but one certainly would, and I would smoke it before the day was over.

I did not, however, wish to be found dead as I was now. Once the mere rumour of Monsieur Zenith had been enough to galvanise the police forces of the world into action, but now? Would my remains even be recognised, or would I be simply another nameless soul, unknown and unmourned? It should not concern me, I know, but even I am capable of a certain vanity now and again. I could at least look the part and give some doddering geriatric amongst the London police force a chance to recall the glory days of his own youth, and my own.

I leaned forward and provided the taxicab driver with a new destination.

The Black Museum – a second rate collection of nefarious heirlooms gathered by third rate police officers – at New Scotland Yard had been in existence longer even than I. I had never visited it before but it was simplicity itself to make enquiries at the reception desk and then walk confidently upstairs to its wooden door.

The rather pretty girl at reception had told me that the curator had gone for lunch, and so I had the run of the place. It was not, truth be told, exactly the sort of place I cared to spend an idle half hour, but I knew that certain of my own possessions were housed somewhere within and so the effort was worthwhile, I judged. Specifically, I knew that – following one particular misadventure shortly before I left for the East – my cloak, cane and hat had been handed over to be exhibited at the Museum. An honour of sorts, but one which I intended to reject, these several decades later.

Through the wooden door was an outer room, a cluttered hodge-podge of a place, more consistent with the lost-and-found in a poorly-maintained country station than a museum supposedly funded by the British Government. A full-size gallows dominated a dark corner, hiding part of one wall covered in photographs of the hanged, while a large table on which were displayed a variety of murderous looking weapons took up most of the floor space. Here and there tall containers were scattered, seemingly at random, umbrella stands holding not umbrellas but brightly polished blades, sword sticks, and heavy wooden clubs and coshes. A dressmaker's dummy, wearing a brown suit punctured with bullet holes, stood just inside the door, alongside a glass topped cabinet filled with faded letters and pages clipped from newspapers, each the record of some terrible crime or other. Of my clothing there was no sign.

I crossed the room and tried the door to the inner part of the Museum but it was locked and I had foolishly not come prepared for breaking and entering. I was just considering putting my shoulder to the door, clumsy and primitive though that approach might be, when I heard footsteps from the other side and saw the handle of the door turn.

In an instant I had secreted myself behind the gallows, from which position I watched as an elderly Police Constable, presumably the Curator, stepped into the room with a puzzled expression on his face. I could have remained hidden but one old man was unlikely to cause me any great difficulty and, besides, he might have information which could be of use to me. I stepped out and, in the same movement, grabbed and unsheathed one of the sword-sticks, before applying the edge of the blade to the man's throat.

Even in such socially awkward situations, I see no call for rudeness. 'I wonder,' I whispered in his ear, 'if you could assist me?'

The man nodded, carefully, and I continued. 'I am looking for a specific item. One which was, at one time, part of this excellent collection. A black cloak and top hat, with a cane to complete the ensemble, each marked with the letter 'Z'. They were,' I concluded, 'the property of the infamous Monsieur Zenith.'

Sadly, the policeman remained silent and I was momentarily chagrined at his failure to hold up his end of the conversation, until I noticed that I had been pressing rather harder than I intended and the blade had cut his skin in a long, scarlet line. Not deadly, by any manner of means, but clearly enough to discourage the flow of gentlemanly discourse. I eased back a little, and the man gave a long, heavy breath before speaking.

'Zenith, you say?' he finally managed. 'Can't say I recognise the name. But I can check the records for you. Wouldn't be a problem at all.'

His lack of recognition was a disappointment but his desire to help was heart-warming. I lowered the blade a little and gestured for him to check the records as he saw fit. He moved surprisingly quickly across to the glass topped cabinet and pulled open a series of drawers built into its body. I cursed myself for having missed them for, within a minute at most, he had the information I required.

He coughed and, without taking his eyes from the sword tip I had pointed at his throat, read from a folder he had open in his hands. 'Costume of Monsieur Zenith, comprising silk opera cloak (black), matching silk hat (black) and ebony cane (engraved 'Z' on the pommel). Sold at auction, 3 July 1968'.

'Costume!' I cried angrily, losing control of my temper for just a second. 'And what do you mean, sold? Explain yourself!'

I was ashamed to see the old man stumble backwards into the cabinet in the face of my anger and immediately moderated my tone. 'Why were these garments sold? Does it say?'

'No longer required, it says here,' he said, 'Not criminally significant.'

I had learned a lesson from my previous outburst and retained my temper, even in the face of such gross provocation.

'And does it also say to whom the garments were sold?' I asked, mildly, then listened with interest to his reply before bundling him, unconscious, into one of his own cupboards.

II.

I must say that at first glance I admired the taste of this Zachary Slade very much. Even apart from his having purchased my own elegant accoutrements, the stately home in Hampshire he had made his base looked quite splendid as I admired it in the fading evening light.

Fortunately the new high speed trains had made light work of the journey from London, and I was able to position myself just outside one window, looking in at a deserted drawing room, as the sun set behind some distant hills. The museum curator had told me that this Slade had purchased my possessions along with those of sundry others. They would be worn by Slade, he said, in his stage persona as Zachary of *Zachary and the Zephyrs*, a 'rock' band of some renown, apparently. The man was in residence this evening, which was not ideal, but for obvious reasons I needed to regain the cloak, hat and cane before the day was out. I had but four cigarettes left and with the removal of each subsequent one the danger of premature death became all the greater.

I pressed my tip of my walking-stick into a tiny gap at the base of the window and, with some difficulty, pushed it open, then cocked a leg over the sill, preparatory to entry. I was just about to swing the other over when the door to the room swung open and a tribe of unwashed gypsy types flooded in. Fortunately, a silk screen lay close to hand and I was able to slip behind it — the second time

I had been forced to hide like a common burglar in a single day! —
before anyone noticed my presence.

As I crouched behind the screen and listened, it quickly became
clear that rather than a tribe of Romany travellers, this motley
ensemble was Mr Slade's entourage. Someone turned a
gramophone on and the air was filled with the most painful sound,
assaulting my eardrums with the force of a thousand demented
banshees. I have seen the most horrific tortures in my long life, but
frankly nothing struck me as so brutalising to the senses as that
sonic attack. I freely admit that even I, Zenith, nearly took to my
heels, preferring the risk of capture to enduring that noise for even
a second more. But just as I felt I could take no more, the volume
decreased as the door opened again and someone I could not quite
see entered the room. From the murmured greetings I heard,
however, there could no doubt that this was Zachary Slade himself,
come to join his companions.

It has never been my way to take the safe route through life.
Take no foolish risks, certainly, and always think before you act, but
act nonetheless, for nobody has ever achieved his goals by simply
sitting around and doing nothing. So it was that I stepped out from
behind the screen and, taking in the scene as I did so, bowed low to
the room.

To my surprise, Slade was actually dressed in my cloak and hat,
and carrying my cane. I could see the golden Z on the pommel of
the cane, a little tarnished but recognisable all the same. An
attractive young woman was holding onto his arm as though she
would fall otherwise. Her eyes were heavy lidded and partially
closed, with what I of all people recognised as the half-living daze
of the confirmed opium addict. There was a fragile beauty about
her; nonetheless, with her fine blonde hair brushing her bare
shoulders and the thin white dress she wore accentuating her
figure most appealingly. He, on the other hand, ran a little to fat
and his own blond hair was almost artificial in its sheen. He had
very pale blue eyes and a tiny scar above the left side of his mouth,
causing his upper lip to rise marginally at one end, so that he
seemed permanently to be smirking at something unseen. A hand-

155

rolled cigarette dangled limply from his mouth, emitting an evil smell, which I took to be marijuana.   His home might be rather elegant, but I suspected that he and I would not be close friends and that it might in fact be easier simply to kill the man and take re-possession of my things.   But for all they were seeming dolts and congenital idiots, Slade's entourage did have the benefit of overwhelming numbers, and it was doubtful than even I could manage to escape should I take such a drastic step.

And so I bowed low once more and announced myself instead.

'Good evening. I am Monsieur Zenith!' I said, and then said no more, knowing that someone would fill the silence and thus provide me with a starting point for whatever it was I chose to do next.   At that point I had no real idea myself, but I was confident something would turn up.

Sure enough, one gentleman in tight silver trousers and with stars painted on his cheeks piped up almost immediately. 'You in the business then?' he asked. 'Name like that, bound to be.'

That will do nicely, I thought.

'Indeed I am,' I said. 'I work as a theatrical agent in the Far East, booking concert tours throughout the region, and arranging for exemplary artistes to visit our most exotic outposts and entertain our most illustrious inhabitants. And I am in the country at the moment hoping to add Zachary and the Zephyrs to our roster of stars!'

I smiled at Slade, who appeared to have taken my entrance in his stride and was now sitting with the girl at his feet, her arms wrapped around his leg.

'Money is no object, Mr Slade, so perhaps we might talk?'

As I had hoped, Slade was amused by my impertinence and beckoned to one of his people to bring me a chair. After I had settled myself, he offered his cigarette to me but I shook my head and offered my opened cigarette case to him in return. 'You might find one of these to your liking,' I said as he took one of my remaining four cigarettes and I another. 'I have them specially made for me in bulk, with the tobacco soaked in opium until it is infused with the stuff. They can be very strong, I should warn you.'

156

Dangerous, I know, both for Slade and myself, but I did not feel my customary energy as I sat there, talking to this fool of a musician and I hungered to make an immediate ending to the matter – the entire matter – one way or the other. But as I watched his eyes glaze and felt my own heartbeat slow to a pleasant rumbling I knew that neither of us had made a deadly choice and that this charade must go on a little longer.

To that end, I suggested to Slade that we leave the communal area and go somewhere quieter and more private to discuss terms for his potential tour. He was amenable, so far as I could tell, for his words were mumbled and indistinct (I would have thought, from my reading of the popular press, that a modern musician would have a stronger head for narcotics) and he and I left the room together, followed by the girl, whose attractiveness waned as she begged Slade for 'a little taste' of something unspecified. He pushed her away and, opening a door seemingly at random, went inside. Obviously, I stopped and gestured for the girl to enter first. I was pleased to see that even in her unfortunate state she recognised courtesy and manners, for she rewarded me with a quite lovely smile, which restored her entirely to my good graces.

I only wish I could say the same of Zachary Slade. From the instant we sat down, with the girl splayed across his lap, he quizzed me offensively about what he called my 'real reasons' for visiting England. At first, I put this down to the well-known insecurity of the artist, for nobody in this country could possibly know who I actually was. But as he continued to attempt to draw the conversation away from matters musical and financial, a worrying thought occurred to me. Why, if Slade had purchased my clothing for his stage act, was he wearing it tonight, when sitting at home with friends? Why, even if he wished to dress up off-stage, did he choose my cloak, hat and cane in particular? And why, now I came to listen to the sounds coming from outside this room, had the music stopped playing?

I may have my faults, but nobody could ever claim I am indecisive. If my fears proved in the end to be misguided, at worst I would relieve Slade of the items I had come to reclaim and, if not, then better to take the initiative than wait for others to act. The thought, as they say, was master to the deed. I stood quickly and pulled the sword from within the stick I had taken from the Black Museum. But even so, perhaps I had waited too long to act, for Slade was quicker still.

Allowing the girl to fall to the floor, where she lay muttering indistinct complaints, Slade pulled a pistol from his pocket, but my own cloak came to my rescue. As he attempted to bring the gun to bear it became tangled in the cloak's silk lining and I was able to bring my sword slicing down through the fabric and across the back of his hand. With a curse he dropped the gun and I moved forward to press my advantage, only to find myself in turn frustrated as he threw the slashed cloak over my sword arm and, with an unexpected speed, struck a double blow to my face. We were too close together now for sword play and I allowed the weapon to drop to the floor, the better to defend myself with my fists. We exchanged blows in equal measure for a moment or two, but I was the greater pugilist and I soon laid him out, though not before he had managed to shout to his confederates for help.

I had just enough time to reach the door and turn the key in the lock before anyone could enter but the heavy thudding I heard from outside the room confirmed that I had little time to waste in making my escape. I gathered up my hat and cane, the cloak now being torn, and tried each of the two large windows in turn. The first had been nailed shut at some point in the past, but the second opened a little as the thumping from outside became louder. The door began to move alarmingly in response to the efforts of those attempting to gain entry. I redoubled my efforts to open the window but it was obvious that no effort of mine would force open a large enough gap to allow my egress. There was no time left, I could see, and poor plan though it was, I realised that my only hope was to take the gun and make what use of it I could. Perhaps I could swap my own freedom for that of Slade and the girl? It was only then that I realised that the gun was nowhere to be seen — nor was the girl!

'Stop right there, Mr Zenith, or I will shoot,' a female voice said from behind me. For an instant I measured the distance to my sword-stick lying on the floor, but it was still tangled in the ripped cloak and for all that I would far prefer death to capture, I had little doubt that the girl was capable of shooting only to wound. Better instead to submit to a temporary loss of freedom, and leave myself whole for some future escape.

I raised my hands and slowly turned. The girl stood with her back to the door and the gun trained on me. She reached behind herself and turned the key in the lock. 'Come on in, boys,' she said. 'Someone phone a doctor for Inspector Grange. He's taken a nasty knock. You,' she gestured in my direction. 'Go with Constable Peters for now. But bear in mind, he doesn't like people who assault his superior officer any more than I do, and you wouldn't be the first thug to be shot while trying to escape.'

To be captured by a woman was ignominious enough, but her dismissive tone added sufficient insult to injury that I could not leave matters as they stood for even a second longer.

'I am no common thug, madam,' I began to explain, but rather than listen she reached up and removed my sunglasses, exposing my pink eyes to the light. She whistled and murmured 'So, it's true after all.'

She handed the glasses back to me.

I made the tiniest of bows in deference to her courtesy.

'You are who you claim to be then?' she asked, but it was evidently a rhetorical question for, before I could answer, she continued, 'My name is Doctor Philly Winton and I work – on occasion – with the police force on the more...unusual type of case. When I opened the door of my flat to you earlier today I admit I was intrigued. The person you were looking for is not the sort of man to attract casual visitors, which is one reason I was delighted to take up residency there when he allowed his own tenancy to lapse. But when I circulated your description to friends in the Met, the only name they could suggest was a man believed dead decades ago.'

In case I had not drawn the obvious conclusion, she reached up and pulled the blonde wig from her head and threw it on a nearby table. Now that her natural mousey brown hair was exposed and her eyes no longer half shut in an opiate trance, I recognised the woman I had taken for a maid that morning. I bowed again in mixed admiration and recognition and (I admit it, gladly) because she was a beautiful woman.

She continued, 'I would probably have forgotten all about it, but this afternoon I heard about a very similar looking man who had visited the Black Museum at Scotland Yard and knocked out the old lad who keeps an eye on the exhibits. And when that elderly officer came to and explained that his assailant had been enquiring after the very same apparently deceased individual, well...let's just say that in light of certain unfortunate and on-going drug possession charges the real Mr Slade was delighted to give the Constabulary the run of his house for this little operation. I have no idea where you sprang from, Mr Zenith, or how you manage to look so young for a man in his mid-nineties, but I'm sure we can sort that out later, back at the station.'

She motioned to the officer assigned to me and, with a gun aimed at me the entire time, he escorted me from the room.

It seemed that for all her bravado, Dr Winton had not been entirely as confident of my capture as she claimed, for there was no police van waiting outside for me, and one had to be called, necessitating a brief wait.

In the meantime I was to be handcuffed and incarcerated in a small pantry on the ground floor, with the door firmly locked and my police guard unwavering in keeping his gun pointed at me. He was a man of disappointingly few words, and failed to engage in any of the several stimulating topics of conversation I instigated. All the while, my brain was working feverishly, checking one escape stratagem after another, each as futile and doomed to failure as the last. I had at most fifteen minutes before the van arrived and, if need be, I knew that I could at least rush him and, at this close range, be fairly certain of a fatal wound. Better, far better, to lose my life than my freedom, for the one is essential to the other in the mind of any sane man. Better yet, though, to choose my own end.

'Would you object if I smoked?' I asked, pulling out my cigarette case with some difficulty. There being no objection, I took one and offered the last in the case to my jailor. 'Would you care for one?' I said, and laughed. 'Don't worry, I have plenty more.'

The man took the cigarette then, as I went to light it, pulled my own from my mouth and handed the other back to me. 'This works better for me, mate,' he said with what I presume he intended as a cruel smile. 'As you wish,' I replied and lit them both, inhaling deeply.

Was it disappointment I felt as the familiar warmth of the opium washed over me? I think not, though I did feel a certain satisfaction in watching the policeman's mouth gape open and his eyes roll back in his head. His body had not even fallen fully back in his chair before I had the keys to the handcuffs out of his pocket. The small pantry window would be a squeeze and might cause some scuffing to the brim of my top hat, but other than I felt more alive than I had in thirty years. I pictured the look on the delightful Dr Winton's face when she discovered me gone and felt sure that we would soon meet again.

I had believed I was bored. In that I was mistaken. Perhaps there was something in this London of 1971 which was fresh and new and interesting after all...